God's Mailbox

God's Mailbox

More Stories about Stories in the Bible

MARC GELLMAN

Illustrated by
DEBBIE TILLEY

MORROW JUNIOR BOOKS
New York

1   2   3   4   5   6   7   8   9   10

Library of Congress Cataloging-in-Publication Data
Gellman, Marc.
God's mailbox: more stories about stories in the Bible/by Marc Gellman.
p. cm.
Summary: A collection of humorous stories derived from the Old Testament.
ISBN 0-688-13169-7
[1. Humorous stories.]   I. Title.
PZ7.G28355Go 1996   [Fic]—dc20
95-14894   CIP AC

For the children of my children's children,
so that they will have something more from me than
just the color of my eyes.

My Thanks

....

To Rabbi David Shapiro, who taught me midrash and then everything.

To the children of my synagogue, who, each month at the family service, have giggled their views into this book.

To my dear friend Marilyn Levy, who knew that although nothing is ever good enough, some things are good enough to let go.

To my editors, David Reuther and Ellen Dreyer at Morrow Junior Books, who had both the tact and wisdom to say to me at appropriate moments in the preparation of this book, "It's probably just me, but I have no idea at all what you are trying to say here."

To Sara Friedlander, who loves midrash, spooky stories, and Broadway musicals, and who was the only other human being, besides me, who liked the title *Ox Drool Bread.*

To Larry Hurwitz, who has understood exactly how important modern midrash is to making a vibrant Jewish future and securing the Jewish past, but who definitely would have been the one with his hand raised at the bottom of Mt. Sinai, asking Moses, "Does that come on disk?"

To Sheldon Fogelman, who has the most profoundly deep and incredibly wise understanding of how to get tuna fish.

To Betty, who sees all, changes little, and lets me fly to a place where everything is clear and kind, naive and expectant, gentle and funny, and very close to The Place…

Contents

....

Author's
Note

. . . .

This book is filled with stories *about* stories in the Bible. I put the chapters and verses of the Bible stories after each of my stories and in the table of contents so you can know which story in the Bible each of my stories is about. Some of my stories are funny. I couldn't help this, but don't be tricked: I also tried to put some serious stuff inside every funny thing. It's kind of like eating chocolate-covered cherries. You start out thinking that you are just eating a piece of chocolate when suddenly— *yikes!*—your mouth tells you that you just ate a cherry, too!

Some of these are funny stories with a serious cherry inside, and some of them are serious stories with a funny cherry inside. All of them are more than you think, and that's the way it is with the Bible. You may think you are reading some simple story about Adam and Eve when suddenly—*yikes!*—you realize that it is a big and deep story about all men and all women who ever lived. The Bible stories are like that. Every chocolate has a cherry inside.

To write stories *about* stories in the Bible, you have to love the Bible, you have to love God, and you have to love people. I am usually three for three, although some days I am only two for three. Those are the days I give up on people. This usually happens after I see the stuff on the evening news. Anyway, if you don't love the Bible, you won't want to figure out what all the stories in it really mean. And if you don't love God, you won't be able to see how the Bible is—somehow, someway—*the way God has talked to us*. And if you don't love people, you won't understand that the Bible is the way people can best learn how to live together. The Bible is kind of like a pair of glasses through which I look at the world. I see our stories in its stories. I see all of us in all of them, and most of all I see God there and I see God here.

I am a rabbi, and the first rabbis who wrote stories about stories in the Bible called their stories *midrashim*. The old midrashim are almost as old as the Bible, which means that as soon as there was a Bible, there were stories about the stories in the Bible. The Bible has our best stories, and it has always brought out our best questions. Some of those questions became midrashim, and some just stayed questions.

The stories in this book are modern midrashim. I have been writing and telling modern midrashim for over twenty years. This is my second book of such stories. The first one was called *Does God Have a Big Toe?* (to find out you have to read the book). I hope that this book will make you want to write your own modern midrashim. All you need is something to write with and a few good questions about the stories in the Bible. You can lose the stuff you write with, but *please* don't lose your questions. Your questions are a part of every story in the Bible. Maybe your answers to your questions will become new stories about the stories in the Bible. Maybe they will teach somebody something about Adam, Eve, Noah, Abraham, Isaac, Jacob, Rebekah, Rachel, Leah, or the bush that was burning but did not burn up—something that nobody ever knew before.

So don't lose your questions about the stories in the Bible. They are like the cherry inside the chocolate. They are the reason God made Moses schlepp up to the top of Mount Sinai to get all this for all of us.

If I were a singer, I would sing about the Bible. If I were a painter, I would paint about the Bible. If I were a dancer, I would dance about the Bible. And if I were a balloon maker, I would send up one humongous balloon that would have these words on it:

READ THE BIBLE RIGHT AWAY! If you do, something great will happen. You will find hope for when your hope has died. You will find joy for when you are sad. You will find words that teach you the right way to live when you are not doing the right thing. You will find words that teach you how to slow down when you are moving too fast, and words to help you remember to say "Thank you!" at least twice as often as you say "Gimme!" And you will find stories about talking snakes, big floods, frogs that fall from the sky, and a bunch of other really funny and really goofy and really wonderful stories that people have loved for about four thousand years. (Yep! That is just about how old the Bible is!) SO GET GOING AND START READING THE BIBLE RIGHT AWAY!

I know that's a lot of words to write on one balloon, but I *said* it would be one humongous balloon.

God bless us one and all!

Smack the Coconut

Smack the
Coconut

....

Adam loved to play games, and the animals in the Garden of Eden loved to play games, but the games they loved to play were different—really different!

The animals loved to play games like chase your tail, but Adam didn't like that game, because he didn't have a tail. Adam loved playing smack the coconut, where he would take a big stick and try to hit a coconut over the wall that went around the garden, but most of the animals didn't like that game, because they didn't have hands to hold a stick. Besides, they thought the game was a waste of a perfectly good coconut that you could eat instead of smack.

The animals loved to play I'm gonna bite your neck, but after playing that game once with some tigers and bears, Adam decided that he would never play this game with any animal that had pointy teeth! Adam loved to play hit the little white ball into a hole in the ground with a curved stick, but the animals thought this game was so silly it would never catch on.

The animals loved to play pull on both ends of a rope with your teeth, but every time Adam played that game with some big strong animal, he got dragged around the garden by his teeth.

The animals loved the games where they got to eat something or chase something or bite something, and Adam loved the games where he got to hit something or catch something or run or jump somewhere. In fact, there was only one game both Adam and the animals loved to play. That game was called jump and run around and make all kinds of happy noises for no reason at all. So both Adam and the animals loved to play games, but it was hard for them to play together.

God knew what was wrong. God had put lots of animals in the garden but only one person. God knew that Adam was lonely. Of course there was a reason why God made just one person to begin with. God didn't want any person to say, "My family is better than your family." God wanted to make all the families come from the same person so that everybody would feel special to God in the same way. This was a very good reason for God, but it was a very bad deal for Adam, because it meant that if he didn't want to play chase your tail, or I'm gonna bite your neck, he had to play all by himself. So God decided to make Adam somebody to play with. But God knew that it was also time for things to change.

The next day Adam woke up and screamed, "*Yeouch!*" He was real sore on his left side.

God told Adam why he was sore. "Adam, you are sore in your side because last night that's where I took the stuff to make another person to share the garden with you. I made her from your rib so that you will not argue about who is better. I want all people to remember that everybody came from you, and you came from me. I did all this so that you and the woman could become a family and make babies, and that way I can get out of the people-making business. Most of all, I did this so that you will not be lonely anymore."

"Where's the person?" Adam asked while rubbing his side, but God was finished talking. Adam looked all over the garden to find the other person, but all he found was a few animals that wanted to play I'm gonna bite your neck.

Later in the day the pain went away from Adam's side, and after a while he forgot he had ever been sore. He headed out to the field in the afternoon to play a little smack the coconut, and, as usual, none of the animals wanted to play. So, as usual, Adam played alone. He grabbed his favorite stick, threw a nice big coconut up into the air, and took a big swing at it with the stick. *Smack!* The coconut sailed high into the sky, but just before the coconut whizzed over the wall of the garden, a hand reached up from the weeds and caught the coconut! Adam couldn't believe his eyes.

"Nice hit!" a voice shouted from the outfield. It wasn't an elephant voice. It wasn't a monkey voice. It wasn't a hippopotamus voice. It was a voice like his voice, only a little higher and a little softer.

"Who's out there?" Adam asked. That's when Adam saw that the voice was attached to a hand, and the hand was attached to another person. It was the other person! The other person kind of looked like him except that her hair was longer and she had curves where he had bumps. Adam was happy right away.

The other person handed him the coconut, and Adam said, "Thank you."

The other person said, "You're welcome."

Adam said, "What's your name?"

The other person said, "What's a name?"

Adam said, "A name is a word we can use to find each other. My name is Adam, which God told me means 'red earth,' because God made me out of red earth. If you can't find me, all you have to do is call out my name, and wherever I am, I'll come running to find you again."

"What did God use to make me?" the other person asked.

"God made you out of one of my bones," Adam answered.

"Well then, maybe my name should be Bony," the other person said.

"Bony is a good name," said Adam.

"Would you teach me how to smack the coconut?" Bony asked.

Adam said, "Sure!"

Adam was thrilled and delighted to find out that Bony loved to play games as much as he did. Best of all, she loved the same games Adam loved, except the game where you try to hit the little white ball into a hole in the ground with a curved stick. Bony agreed with the animals that this was such a silly game nobody would ever want to play it.

Adam and Bony played smack the coconut all the rest of the day. Then all the animals in the garden crept forward into the field to say hello to the new person God had put in the garden. The animals were a little disappointed that she didn't have a tail, but they liked her, and she liked them.

Then, as the sun was setting over the edge of the garden wall, Adam and Bony and all the animals in the Garden of Eden got together and played the one game they all loved to play: jump and run around and make all kinds of happy noises for no reason at all. Except that on that day there were lots of reasons to be happy.

After Adam and Bony left the Garden of Eden, Bony had babies, and because of this, Adam started calling Bony by the name Eve, which God told them meant "the mother of all peoples." Bony liked the name Eve. But the main thing for both of them was not their names. The main thing was not being lonely because they had somebody to love.

—Genesis 2:18–22

When You're Shaking, Hug a Bear!

....

Adam and Eve were dumb, but it wasn't really their fault. Because both of them were made by God, they had no mother and no father to teach them how to do things. Sometimes even people with mothers and fathers grow up dumb because they don't listen to their parents, but Adam and Eve never had a chance.

Adam and Eve had nobody to teach them to chew with their mouths closed, nobody to teach them how to ride a bike, nobody to teach them how to open a box of cereal, nobody to teach them how to fasten their seat belts, and nobody to remind them to look both ways before they crossed the street. Adam and Eve had nobody to tie their shoes or wrap a scarf around their necks on a cold day in the garden. They had nobody to tuck them into bed at night, nobody to sing to them, and nobody to tell them stories about cows jumping over the moon. And in the middle of the night, they had nobody they could ask for a glass of water when what they really wanted was not a glass of water but somebody to sleep next to so that the thing they thought was under the bed would not bite them. Adam and Eve had to figure out everything by themselves.

It all started the very first day God made them. Adam got a funny feeling inside of him. He asked Eve if she felt okay, but she said, "Something inside me hurts, too. I wonder what's wrong." Then they saw a monkey eating a banana. "Maybe we should do that," Eve said. And so they both ate some bananas, and the hurt inside them went away. They figured out right away that eating was a good way to stop the inside hurt. They *really* liked eating, so they ate some pears and apples, a few oranges, several mangoes, a papaya or two, a bunch of pineapples, and a whole load of coconuts. Then they both burped a lot.

Adam said, "I've got it! When we feel the inside hurt, that means we should eat till we burp."

Then it began to rain in the garden. Adam and Eve had no idea what rain was. They just stood there, looking up at the gray sky and getting soaked, not knowing what to do. "The sky is leaking!" Adam said to Eve.

Then they saw a huge elephant. The elephant was so big that, underneath the elephant, it was dry. Adam and Eve ran to the place under the elephant, and they stopped getting wet.

Eve said, "I get it. When the sky is leaking, stand under an elephant."

Standing under the elephant in the cold rain with no clothes on was a new feeling for Adam and Eve, but it was not a good feeling. They were dry, but they were shaking all over. They couldn't feel the tips of their toes or the ends of their fingers. "Wh-Wh-What's wrong now?" said Adam.

"I d-d-don't know," said Eve. "Maybe elephants are good for stopping sky leaks but not so good for stopping the sh-sh-shakes."

Just then Eve and Adam saw a big brown bear walk into a cave. They followed the bear and saw him curl up into a big furry ball. They touched the bear, and he felt so soft and warm that they curled up with him and hugged him tight. (I told you they were dumb!) Right away they stopped shaking. Soon Adam and Eve could feel their fingers and toes again.

Eve said, "I get it. When you're shaking, hug a bear!"

Late that night, Adam and Eve were walking around the garden. But as they were walking, their eyes kept closing, and they would bump into trees. "What's wrong now?" Eve said, yawning. Then they saw a cat

curled up on some soft grass. The cat had its eyes closed, and it was breathing softly. "That looks good to me," said Eve. She lay down on the grass, closed her eyes, and was soon breathing softly.

"I get it," Adam said to himself. "When our eyes start to close, and we start to bump into trees, that means we should fall down on soft grass and close our eyes all the way." He did it, too, and soon Adam and Eve were fast asleep.

The next morning, when Adam's eyes opened, he felt great, but when he looked around, Eve was gone. Adam had no idea where Eve could be. It was the first time they had ever been apart from each other. Adam felt something new that morning. It was a hurt inside him, but it was not like the inside hurt that made him eat until he burped. It was not like the hurt in his toes that made him want to look for a bear to hug. This was a hurt that came from all over his insides. Little drops of salty water were dripping from his eyes. Adam screamed, "Eve, where are you? I hurt all over!"

But he still could not see Eve.

Adam saw mother and father frogs croaking with their baby frogs. He saw mother and father monkeys picking bugs out of the hair of their baby monkeys. He saw mother and father elephants eating grass together with their baby elephants. He saw mother and father eagles looping the loop in the blue sky together with their little baby eagles. Everywhere Adam looked, he saw families. Then Adam cried out in a voice bigger than he had ever known he had, "Eve! I miss you! I don't want to be alone! I want to be with you! And I want babies to be with us, too! I want to be a family! I love you, Eve! It hurts me in a deep place when you're not here!"

At just that moment, Eve walked out of the bushes, carrying a big bunch of bananas. "You don't have to yell!" she said, smiling. "I'm not deaf, you know!"

Then Adam said, "I get it! When we're lonely, we need to get near somebody we love right away." Adam hugged Eve and said, "I love you, Eve!"

Eve hugged Adam and said, "I love you, Adam!" And from that moment on, they were never dumb again.

—*Genesis 2:21–23*

Adam and
Raoul

....

Some people just work all the time and never really rest. Some of them have to work all the time because they are poor or because they have really hard jobs, and that is bad. But some people who work all the time don't have to but do it anyway, and that is stupid!

Adam was one of those people who could not wait to get up in the morning to work. He worked all day, every day, all the time. To help him get up extra early in the morning, Adam used a rooster named Raoul. Raoul was the first alarm clock.

Every morning all the animals would be awakened by Raoul's very loud "Cock-a-doodle." (Another thing not many people know is that in those days roosters knew only cock-a-doodle. Roosters didn't learn to cock-a-doodle-DOO until years later.) Anyway, not only was Raoul's cock-a-doodle very loud, but he would fly right over to each animal and cock-a-doodle each animal right in its ear so that it would jump straight up in the air. Adam loved Raoul's cock-a-doodling because it helped him get up real early and work even longer, but the other animals in the Garden of Eden were not big fans of Raoul. The night animals especially hated Raoul because his cock-a-doodling would wake them up just as they were beginning their sleep for the day.

The owls and the raccoons and the bats and the other night animals asked Adam to tell Raoul to shut up, but Adam didn't listen to them. He just said, "Got to go to work now!" So the night animals decided to kidnap Raoul.

That night the lion snuck up on Raoul, pounced on him, and stuffed

him into his mouth. But just as the lion was about to swallow Raoul, Adam woke up and screamed at the lion, "Give me back Raoul, right now!" The lion spat out Raoul, who bounced against a tree and ran away.

The next morning Adam slept right through the sunrise and woke up very upset. "Oh, no! I've lost two hours of work. Where is Raoul?" But Raoul the rooster was nowhere to be found. At first Adam thought that Raoul had flown away, out of the garden. Then Adam thought, Maybe the lion caught him again and swallowed. Adam was very upset. "How can I get up early, now that Raoul is gone?"

Then God came to him and said, "Listen, Adam, we need to talk. I made you strong and I made you a good worker and I am happy for that, but I did not make you strong enough to work all the time. You need to rest and play and read and find ways to thank me for all the good things I have given you. Resting is just as important as working. How about this? You work as hard as you want for six days, but rest on the seventh day."

Adam thought, One day out of seven is not that bad. Adam said to God, "I'll do it, but I won't like it."

God said, "Try it, you'll like it." Adam tried it. And Adam liked it. Adam finally realized that resting is a very good thing.

Raoul came back after a few days. Adam was happy and Raoul was happy, and even the other animals in the garden were happy, because while he was gone, Raoul had learned an amazing thing. He had learned how to do a very soft cock-a-doodle that did not wake up anybody but Adam. This was good for Adam, because he was sure to be able to get up early for work. This was also very good for Raoul, because his soft cock-a-doodle did not wake up the lion, and letting the lion sleep is almost as good an idea as resting on the Sabbath day.

—*Genesis 2:2–3*

What's Holy?

Teaching about what's holy was the hardest thing God had to teach Adam and Eve and their children. Of course God knew what was holy because God *is* holy, but Adam and Eve had no clue. So this is more or less how God tried to explain it to them.

God said, "Adam, I am all holy, and everything I made is part-holy. Of the part-holy things I made, some have a bigger part that's holy than other part-holy things. Do you understand?"

Now, Adam had no idea what God had said, but Adam did not want to look dumb, so Adam said, "You bet, God, I understand. Yes, I do! I surely understand about holy because you just gave me such a fine explanation just now." (Adam was always kissing up to God.)

At the time, God believed Adam and went on to teach Adam other important things, like how to peel a banana, how to keep ants out of his food, and how long to wait before going swimming after he had lunch. What's holy was never discussed again, and this turned out to be a big mistake.

God put a tree in the middle of the Garden of Eden and told Adam not to eat its fruit because the tree was holy. When Eve came along and wanted to eat from the tree, Adam told her that the tree was holy. Eve said, "How can fruit be holy? Leafy things are not holy. Only living-breathing-moving-around things are holy. Everybody knows that!" So Eve ate, and Adam ate, too, because he was never really that sure what was holy and what wasn't. Then God kicked Adam and Eve out of the Garden of Eden because they ate the fruit of the tree that God said not to eat from, and this proved that they had never really learned what was holy.

One day Adam was tilling a cornfield when he came upon a mouse nibbling on an ear of corn. "Don't eat my corn!" Adam shouted at the mouse, who had not yet learned to be afraid of people. Adam was lifting up his hoe to squash the mouse when Eve stopped him, saying, "Don't kill the mouse! It is a living-breathing-moving-around thing and it is holy."

But Adam said, "Living-breathing-moving-around things are not holy. Only living-breathing-moving-around-things-who-talk are holy." Then Adam squashed the mouse with the hoe. After that, God made farming hard for Adam because Adam still did not know what was holy.

One day Cain and Abel, the two children of Adam and Eve, were grown-up and doing their work. Cain was a farmer, and Abel was a shepherd. They both had a very good year, so they both brought presents for God, to say thank you. Cain brought some old rotted vegetables, thinking, I need my good stuff more than God needs my good stuff. Abel brought his best sheep, thinking, God is the best, so I want to give God the best. God picked Abel's present, and this made Cain very angry.

Cain picked up a sword and was about to kill his brother, Abel, when Abel screamed, "*Stop!* Don't kill me! I'm your brother. I'm a living-breathing-moving-around-thing-who-talks. I am holy."

But Cain said, "Don't be silly! Living-breathing-moving-around-things-who-talk are not holy, only living-breathing-moving-around-things-who-talk-and-don't-get-in-my-way are holy." And so Cain killed his brother, Abel.

That was the first time a person killed another person, and God was very angry. God thought, There is nobody left who knows what's holy. I will have to start again and put some new people in the world who know what's holy. I will just flood the world and start fresh.

Now, God was just about to start the big flood when God saw Noah. Noah's son was about to kill a bird, and Noah yelled at him, "Don't kill

that bird! The bird is a living thing, and being a living thing makes it special, like God. The bird is holy.

"Son, only God is *all* holy. Everything else is part-holy, but being part-holy is good enough. Even rocks have a small part of them that's holy, because even the rocks were made by God. The animals have a bigger part of them that's holy than the rocks have, because they are alive and the rocks aren't. People are even more part-holy than the rocks and the animals, because people are made by God *and* are alive *and* have souls.

"What this means is that you can pick up a rock and throw it for any old reason. But you can kill that bird only if you are starving and need food to eat, and you can't hurt people or kill people unless they are trying to kill you and you can't get away. Being holy is a very good thing, and you should treat everything in the world with love and respect, because holy is the way God touches the world."

Right then and there God decided to save Noah and his family. God realized that even though teaching what is holy is hard, and even though there will always be some people who just don't get it, there will always be some people who do, and they need all the help they can get.

—*Genesis 3:1–7,17; 4:1–16; 6:5–8*

God, Do You
Know How I Feel?

....

In the middle of the Garden of Eden there was a big tree that had on it a big sign with big letters: DON'T EVEN THINK OF EATING THE FRUIT FROM THIS TREE. Of course, when Adam and Eve ate from the fruit of that tree, God kicked them out of the garden right away, which proves that if God puts up a sign, you'd better read it!

Life outside the garden was pretty hard. In the garden most every tree had fruit, most every day was sunny, and most every animal was nice. But outside the garden, lots of trees had bugs, lots of days were cold, and lots of animals wanted to bite, sting, or squash Adam and Eve.

Because of all the hard, cold, biting stuff that was *outside* the garden, Adam was sure that God lived only *inside* the garden. Adam was sad about not living near God anymore, but most days Adam was just too busy to be sad. Adam had to spend a lot of time in the fields plowing, and sowing seed, and keeping the weeds away, and watching out for animals with sting or bite potential. But whenever Adam wasn't busy, he was sad. Really sad.

In the garden, Adam would sometimes sit all day, talking to God. Adam would talk to God about the sky and the water, about the mountains and the valleys. But the thing that Adam talked about most with God was his feelings. Adam would see a beautiful sunset, a perfect flower, a fine spiderweb, a bird with colored feathers, or little fish in the pond, and then Adam would smile this huge smile that seemed to come from his toes and wrap around his face and make his whole body shine.

And Adam would try to explain to God just how he felt seeing such beautiful things all around him.

Sometimes Adam could not find the right words to explain how he felt, and he would just throw up his hands and ask, "God, do you know how I feel?"

Then God would answer in a still, small voice, "I know how you feel." Then God would kiss Adam with a breath of wind, and the two of them would go their separate ways until the next day. Now that Adam was outside the garden, he remembered those talks with God. He was afraid that they would never happen again, and he was very sad.

One day in the fields, Adam saw a sunset that was pretty. It was not quite as red and purple and orange and yellow as the sunsets in the garden, but it was nice. Adam threw up his hands and hollered into the sky, "God, do you know how I feel?" But Adam heard nothing.

Another day Adam came upon a flower. There were not as many flowers outside the garden, but this was a beautiful red one with yellow inside. Adam smelled the flower and smiled. Adam shouted, "God, do you know how I feel?" But still Adam heard nothing.

One morning Adam came upon a spiderweb, and though it was not as big and fine as the spiderwebs in the garden, it was covered with dewdrops that sparkled in the morning light. Adam cried, "God, do you know how I feel?" But Adam heard nothing.

One day Adam saw a flock of geese flying somewhere, and he yelled at the geese, "Come back here, birds! Tell me where you are going. Tell me about the sky and what it's like to fly and how it is to live in a place with no walls, and I will tell you how I feel." But the geese didn't stop, and Adam heard nothing but their honking as they flew off into the gray sky.

Then one day Adam came to the edge of a clear blue pond. Near the water's edge there was a school of little fish swimming around. Adam sat down on a rock, put his head into his hands, and started to cry. First it was a little cry, but soon his whole body was heaving and shaking, and

his tears were dripping into the pond like rain. Each teardrop scared the little fish as it hit the water, but they swam back to him when the water became still again.

Soon Adam stopped crying. He looked at the fish and said nothing. Just then the sun came out from behind a cloud, warming his face. A breath of wind blew against his cheeks and dried his tears, and all of a sudden a still, small voice said, "I know how you feel."

"God, is that you?" Adam asked. "Do you live out here?"

God said, "I live everywhere you let me in."

"I called to you so many times," Adam said. "Why didn't you answer me?"

God said, "I was always answering you. It's just that outside the garden you have to listen a little harder to hear me. Things are not as quiet out here."

"I miss the garden," said Adam.

"I know how you feel," said God. "I am sorry I had to kick you out. Everything was good there, but maybe it was *too* good. The garden was a little small, and you didn't have to work for anything. Even though things are harder outside the garden, you will appreciate what you have. Also, there are no walls out here, and you are needed to make things grow and work. Being in a place that's perfect may not be as good for you as being in a place where you are needed. Outside the garden your children's children's children can grow up and spread out and fill this great big earth. Come to think of it, I'm not really sure which is better—being in the garden or being outside the garden."

Then Adam smiled and said to God, "I know just how you feel."

And God kissed Adam with a breath of wind.

—Genesis 3:23

Painting People
Purple

....

When God was in the middle of making the world, God would get the idea for a new fish or bird or insect or furry animal. Then God would draw an outline of the thing on a piece of paper and clip it to a rope with a clothespin. Angels would pull on the rope and take the piece of paper down to a big building with many rooms. There was a huge sign over the front door to this building that read: THIS IS THE PLACE WHERE WE MAKE ALL THE STUFF GOD THINKS UP.

The first room in this building was the sound room. Here, angels who were good at this sort of thing would think up what sound the fish or bird or insect or furry animal should make. The fish and insects shared the buzzing, humming, clicking, and glurping sounds, because there were so many different kinds of fish and insects in the world that if they each got a special buzz, hum, click, or glurp, there would be no sounds left for all the furry animals and birds.

For the birds and other animals who did get sounds, the angels liked to give out chirps, squeaks, woofs, and moos. But yowls and gurrs were also very popular. After giving out a whole bunch of chirps, squeaks, woofs, moos, gurrs, and yowls, the angels had to mix some of the sounds together. That's how some animals got chirping squeaks, yowly gurrs, and growling woofs, and moos that sounded more like a hoo than a moo.

After the sounds had been attached, God's design for the fish or bird or insect or furry animal was clipped onto the rope again and pulled along to the coloring room. In the coloring room were angels with paints in every color under the sun. God left it up to these angels to decide

exactly what color paint to use on each living thing. As long as everything got painted, God didn't much care what colors the angels used.

Sometimes two coloring angels who were painting the same animal could not agree on what color paint to use. That's how zebras got their stripes. One angel thought the zebra should be all black and another angel thought the zebra should be all white. The two of them painted the zebra at the same time, and that's why the zebra came out striped. Each animal *really* hoped that when it was getting painted the coloring angels wouldn't have a fight.

Also, on days when there were a lot of living things to paint, the coloring angels would decide to just paint everything black or gray or tan, because that was fast and easy. But if only a few things came down the line to be painted that day, the coloring angels would take their time and go wild with the paint. When God first saw the parrots and the tropical fish and the butterflies, God knew right away that they had all been painted on a slow day in the coloring room.

Then one day the design for the first person came down the rope. All the angels were very excited, because they all knew that this was God's favorite design.

Arguing quickly broke out among the angels in the sound room about what sound the person should make. "Too big to chirp!" said one angel.

"This is a woofer if I ever saw one," said another angel.

A third angel said, "The fiercest animals all gurr. No doubt about it, this thing should gurr!"

Then God spoke to the sound angels. "I want the people I make to take care of all the animals and birds and fish. (The insects can take care of themselves.) So why don't you give my person a voice that can make the sounds of *all* the other animals?" Of course, that's just what the angels in the sound room did. They gave the person a voice so wonderful and ears so good and a brain so smart that people can make any sound, from a woofy gurr to a howly yowl to a moo that sounds like a hoo.

Then the design for the first person left the sound room and got pulled into the coloring room. There was a note taped to the first person's toe that read, *Paint this one your best color, and no fighting! Love, God.* Well, the angels in the coloring room immediately began to argue about what was the best color to paint the first person.

"Black is best," shouted one angel.

"No, tan is best," screamed another.

Angels with paintbrushes full of paint were running up to the person to try to paint it their favorite color.

"Pink!"

"Red!"

"Yellow!"

"Purple!"

"Purple?" everyone asked. "How can you paint people purple?"

The angel who liked purple hid behind some cans of paint as the paint went flying all over the coloring room and all over the first person.

When the screaming died down, the coloring room was a mess and the first person was really a mess. Nobody talks about it much, because it was so goofy. The first person came out with one black arm and one tan foot and one yellow toe, along with pink toenails and turquoise hair and violet eyes—a mess!

"I told you not to fight!" God said in a voice loud enough to send all the coloring angels flying to hide behind their paint cans. "Now you have covered my favorite design for a living thing in a hundred colors. About all I can say is that at least you didn't use purple! I am going to have to fix this myself." And with that, the very heavily painted first person whooshed right out of the coloring room and disappeared.

The coloring angels then set about cleaning up the overturned paint cans and paint splashes. Cleaning the coloring room took them most of the day. When they were almost done, a human being came through the door and said, "Can I help?"

The angels could not believe their eyes. There, standing in the doorway of the coloring room, was a fully painted human being with tan skin and yellow hair and blue eyes. Then from the back of the room the angels heard: "I'll help, too!" They whirled around to see another person, this one with black hair and black skin. "Me too," came a voice from the rafters, as a person with brown skin and black hair spoke up. Suddenly the coloring room was filled with freshly painted people in lots of different colors...but each one looked just right. Some had slanted eyes and straight black hair, some had red hair and freckles, some had blue eyes and brown skin. There were people in every shade except purple.

Then God said, "These are only some of the outside colors I will give to people as they start filling up the earth. They will have many different outside colors, but they will all be painted by me. Maybe this way people will learn what you angels forgot: *There is no best color to paint a human being!*

"I want people to love the ways they are different on the outside. I want them to love black and white, short and tall, thin and fat, red and blond, wrinkled and smooth. I made people like snowflakes, only better. No two of them will ever be exactly alike. The different colors may remind them that I gave to each and every one of them a different gift of being good at a different thing, and I need all the different things to make the world run just right.

"But I also want people to remember that underneath the different outside colors they are the same inside. I want them to remember that they all need the same things, that they are all loved by me in the same way, and that nobody is more holy than anybody else. I want them to remember that even though their skin and hair and eyes are different colors, their souls and hearts and needs are just the same. All people need love and respect, rest and fun, soup and salad, bread and bagels, prayers and music. Mostly people need moms and dads who love them always, and they need a few really good friends. All people need these same things, and that is why I am going to paint each of my human beings the *same* colors on the inside."

Then the angels and the freshly painted people just started to cheer and clap and sing and dance, and they all thanked God for being so smart and good and patient. The angels were happy not to have to paint God's favorite design. The people were happy about being painted by God and about having different colors on the outside but the same colors on the inside.

But most of all, they were happy that nobody had been painted purple!

—*Genesis 9:18*

What Does Heaven Look Like?

....

Jacob, who was the son of Isaac and Rebekah, was the kind of person who always wanted to be somewhere else. When he was home, he wanted to be away from home. When he was away from home, he wanted to go home. When he was in a valley, he wanted to be on a mountain, and when he was on a mountain, he wanted to be in a valley. When he was floating down a river, he would be thinking about hiking in the desert. Jacob was just never happy where he was.

One night, after Jacob had left home to go somewhere he thought would be better, he fell asleep and dreamed an amazing dream. Jacob dreamed that he was at the bottom of a tall ladder with its feet on earth and its top in heaven. Angels were climbing up and down on the ladder, but because the ladder was so old and so narrow, so rickety and so wobbly, the angels could not go up and down the ladder at the same time. First some angels had to go all the way up, and then other angels could come all the way down. An angel at the top would wave an orange flag and shout, *"Clear the ladder! Angels coming down!"* When angels wanted to climb back up to heaven, an angel at the bottom would wave an orange flag and yell, *"Clear the ladder! Angels coming up!"* It was a funny system, but it worked.

Jacob saw all this and said to himself, "Heaven is supposed to be a perfect place. I bet I would be happy there. I'm going to climb that ladder and see what heaven looks like." Jacob sneaked up behind a bunch of angels who were waiting their turn to climb up the ladder when the angel at the bottom of the ladder waved his orange flag and yelled,

"Clear the ladder! Angels coming up!" Jacob waited for the last angel in line to start climbing up the ladder, and then he ran to the ladder and started scrambling up just as fast as he could. The climbing-up angels were moving so fast, Jacob just couldn't keep up with them. Soon he was all alone on that rickety old ladder, high in the sky. The ladder was twisting and turning in the wind, and Jacob could barely hang on.

Then Jacob looked up and saw that there was an angel above him on the ladder, climbing down. The angel bumped into Jacob, almost knocking him off the ladder, and shouted, "What the heck are *you* doing here? In fact, who the heck are you?"

"My name is Jacob, and I am a person, and I am climbing this ladder to heaven."

The angel said, "Well, let me tell you something, Mr.-Jacob-person-who-thinks-he-is-climbing-to-heaven. People can't go to heaven until after they die, and then only their souls go, not their bodies. Since you are definitely not dead, you are definitely not getting into heaven today!"

"Oh, please let me see heaven! Please!" Jacob begged the angel. "You have lots of chances to climb down to earth, and this may be my only chance to climb up to heaven."

The angel thought a moment and then said, "Well, you are dreaming all this, which means that your body is still down there on earth, and you are most of the way to heaven already, and climbing down behind you will probably take me more time than letting you climb up the rest of the way.... Oh, all right. I'll let you see heaven. Follow me."

"Yippee!" Jacob said breathlessly, climbing higher and higher on the ladder between heaven and earth.

Finally Jacob made it to heaven. He knew it was heaven for two reasons. Reason 1: It was the place the ladder stopped. And reason 2: There was a big sign that read, THIS IS THE PLACE! WELCOME TO HEAVEN!

Jacob walked over a hill where there was a big light, and that is when he saw it. Heaven was the most beautiful place he had ever seen in his

whole entire life. There were hills and valleys, clean streams and green pastures. Everywhere there were people walking together and talking. Jacob asked the angel, "Who are all these people?"

"They are the souls of people who have died, and when they get to heaven, they meet all the souls of the people they loved who died before them."

"Are there any dogs here?" Jacob asked.

"Sure, there are dogs here," the angel said, laughing, "and cats and parrots and gerbils and hamsters. The ponds are full of goldfish that got flushed down the toilet when the kids weren't looking. But here in heaven the dogs don't chase the cats, the cats don't scratch the furniture, the hamsters don't want to run away, and the goldfish never get flushed."

"Wow," Jacob muttered. Then he said, "I'm hungry from climbing that ladder. Is there anything to eat here in heaven?"

"What's your favorite food?" asked the angel.

"I like wild raspberries," answered Jacob. And—*poof!*—a table with a big bowl of wild raspberries appeared before Jacob. "Neat!" said Jacob as he stuffed his face with the wild raspberries. "All you have to do is wish for something, and you get it right away."

"That's it," said the angel.

No wonder everybody wants to get in here, thought Jacob. He saw a big mountain in the distance and said, "I wonder what it's like on top of that mountain." Then—*whoosh!*—Jacob found himself on the top of the mountain, looking down on the hills and valleys of heaven. "In heaven, all you have to do is want to be someplace, and—*poof!*—you're there right away."

"That's why we don't need cars or trains or planes or bikes up here," said the angel.

"What games do you have up here?" Jacob asked.

"We have all the games you have down on earth, except there's no video games where you zap things. Zapping just isn't allowed in heaven.

There are also no games up here where you can beat somebody or lose to somebody, because winning can make people proud and losing can make people sad, and God does not want people to be either proud or sad in heaven. And, of course, there's no professional wrestling in heaven, because nothing up here is fake."

All Jacob could say was, *"Wow!"* He said *wow* a lot that day.

Jacob spent the next few hours wishing himself from place to place, eating lots of wild raspberries, and playing a kind of tennis game with the angel where they both had to hit the ball very softly over the net and there was no keeping score. After the tennis game, Jacob sat down and put his head in his hands. The angel came over, sat down next to him, and asked, "What's wrong?"

Jacob shrugged his shoulders and said, "I don't know. Everything is really wonderful here in heaven, but I'm just not happy. On earth we have wild raspberries, but they don't just plop into a bowl whenever you want them. You have to find 'em and pick 'em. That's the whole fun of eating wild raspberries. On earth we have mountains, but you can't just wish yourself to the top of them. You have to climb the mountains, and it's the climbing that makes you feel great when you finally get up to the top.

"On earth we have games, but in those games you can win or lose, and it's fun trying to win, and it's good learning how to lose, because you learn to try harder next time. Trying harder the next time is a big thing on earth. Also, I like dogs that chase cats and…I like Wrestlemania. I'm sorry. Heaven is very nice, and I am sure that someday I will be happy to be here, but for now heaven can wait until I have lived my whole life on earth. I want to go home now. I want to go home, I want to go home, I want to…"

Jacob awakened from his dream with a start and looked around. He was glad to be awake, and he was very glad to be alive and back on earth. At first he thought he might still be in heaven, but then he saw a dog run by him chasing a cat, and then he knew that he was back home.

Jacob went to the stream to get some water to splash on his face. There, behind a rock, he thought he saw an orange flag waving, and he thought he heard someone say, "Clear the ladder! Angels coming up!" But when he went to look closer, there was nothing there.

After his dream, Jacob was different. After his dream, Jacob was happy wherever he was. He was happy in the valleys and happy on the mountains; he was happy floating down a river and happy in the desert. Jacob was happy picking raspberries and happy climbing mountains. Jacob was happy just to be alive, and he was happy to know that after he was not alive anymore, there was a place waiting for him that was very good, even if it didn't have Wrestlemania.

—Genesis 28:10–12

The Pharaoh
and the Frog

．．．．．．．．．．．．．．．．．．．．．．．．．．．．．．．．

When Moses told the Pharaoh of Egypt to let all his slaves go free, the Pharaoh of Egypt said to Moses, "What are you, nuts? Let my slaves go free? My slaves are the reason I'm rich. My slaves build my pyramids and my palaces, they harvest my crops, they dig for my gold, they make my bed, they cook my food, they go shopping for me, they get my mail, and they walk my dogs. I'm not going to let them go *anywhere!* What I am going to do, Moses, is throw you out of my palace. Now go tend your sheep or whatever it is you do."

So Moses said to God, "Thanks a lot! Boy, do I feel like a jerk. I walked into the Pharaoh's palace, asked him to let my people go, just like you told me, and the Pharaoh threw me out. God, I can't go back there without some heavy ammunition." God agreed, and the next day Moses appeared again before the Pharaoh.

This time Moses did not say a word. He just put his big walking stick into the pool in the throne room, and *thwack!*—the water in the pool turned to blood. The Pharaoh was amazed and said, "I hate blood!"

He was about to let the Israelites go when his chief magician said, "Turning water into blood is a cinch. Just watch!" Then he turned the water in the Pharaoh's cup into blood.

So the Pharaoh said, "Nice try, Moses, but no cigar! Get out of here right now!" Moses left the Pharaoh's palace to tell God that turning water into blood was good, but not good enough.

The next day Moses returned, and this time God had showed him how to make frogs fall from the sky. The Pharaoh was amazed and again was about to let all the slaves go free when suddenly his magicians plucked their magic twangers and *they* made frogs fall from the sky, too. "You almost tricked me this time," the Pharaoh said as he had Moses and all the frogs thrown out of his throne room.

When everyone had left the palace and the Pharaoh was left alone, he went out onto his balcony to see if the frog rain had stopped. The Pharaoh looked up into the sky when suddenly—*splat!*—a frog fell on his face.

The frog jumped off the Pharaoh's face, onto his shoulder, and croaked in his ear, "Could you please tell me what is going on here? I was just sleeping on my lily pad in my pond, not bothering anybody, when this big wind sucked me up into the air. The next thing I know, I'm sitting on your face looking up your nose. No offense to your face, but I would like directions back to my pond, if you don't mind."

The Pharaoh screamed, *"There's a frog on my face!"* as he rushed out of the throne room. After he washed off the frog slime, he looked in the mirror and said, "I hate blood! And I hate frogs!"

The next day Moses returned to the Pharaoh's palace, but he could not enter the throne room. The Pharaoh had put up posters everywhere in the palace. Each poster had a picture of Moses and a picture of a frog with this message: IF THIS GUY OR THIS FROG SHOWS UP, KICK THEM OUT!

Moses called up to the Pharaoh from the courtyard, "Hey, Pharaoh, watch this!" The Pharaoh peeked out from behind a curtain and saw Moses banging his big walking stick on the ground. With each bang a cloud of fleas rose from the dust and flew everywhere.

The fleas swarmed across Egypt, getting all over everything, including people. Even the Pharaoh started to itch from the fleas that landed on him. He ripped off his clothes and threw them into the pool in his throne room. His clothes landed on the frog, who was sleeping on a lily pad in the pool. The frog woke up with a start and croaked, "Get these stinky Pharaoh clothes off of me!" The Pharaoh was surprised to hear his clothes talking to him, but he soon realized that it was not his underwear talking but the frog who fell from the sky and landed on his face.

The naked Pharaoh ran from the throne room mumbling, "I hate blood. I hate frogs. And I hate fleas!" His servants tried not to look or laugh, but it was real hard, because they just didn't see naked mumbling Pharaohs running away from fleas that often.

The next day, the Pharaoh was bathing in the river to get rid of his fleas when suddenly there was Moses standing in front of him and blowing as hard as he could. Out of Moses' mouth came flies, millions of flies, billions of flies, *gazillions* of flies.

"That's disgusting!" said the Pharaoh as the flies flew out of Moses' mouth and filled the skies all over Egypt. The Pharaoh ran as fast as he could into his throne room and dived into his pool to get away from the flies. When the Pharaoh poked his nose and eyes above the water to see if the bugs had gone away, the frog was snatching flies out of the air with his tongue.

"Want one?" the frog croaked. "Flies are very tasty this time of the year."

The Pharaoh ran from the pool, waving his hands and whining, "I hate blood. I hate fleas. I hate flies. But mostly, I hate frogs!"

The next day the Pharaoh woke up and found out that all his cattle were dead. The Pharaoh slumped down in his throne and cried, "Oh, me! Oh, my! Why are my cows dead?"

Then the Pharaoh heard the frog laughing. "Oh, me! Oh, my!" mimicked the frog. "Why are you such a jerk? Your cows are dead because you were too stubborn to let Moses and his people go free."

The Pharaoh growled, "I am not going to sit here and talk to a frog. Get out of my pool! Get out of my house! Get out of my life!" The Pharaoh ran into his bedroom, slammed the door, and moaned, "I hate blood. I hate frogs. I hate fleas. I hate flies. I hate dead cows! And if that frog says one more word to me, there is going to be one dead frog in Egypt to go along with all my dead cows."

The next day the Pharaoh looked out his window and saw Moses and his brother Aaron picking up ashes from the campfires and throwing them into the air. The Pharaoh laughed. "Oh, Moses, I'm really scared now! Please don't throw dirt!" The Pharaoh was laughing and all his servants were laughing when suddenly a big wind blew the ashes high into the sky. Every little speck of ash that landed on a person turned into a big ugly zit. The Egyptians ran all over, complaining about the plague of zits, especially the teenagers.

The Pharaoh sat down on the edge of his pool, and the frog hopped up on his shoulder and croaked into his ear, "You may be the dumbest man in the whole wide world. You are wrecking your country, killing your cattle, spoiling your people's complexions, and all because you won't let Moses and his people get out of here."

The Pharaoh stood up, grabbed his hair, and yowled, "I am the *Pharaoh*! I am the boss of everybody! I am a god! Nobody tells me what to do—not Moses, not Moses' god, and *definitely* not some smelly old frog! If anybody thinks I am going to let my slaves go free because some of my people have zits, they have another think coming!" Then the Pharaoh stomped off into the next room. His servants heard him say, "Blood, frogs, fleas, flies, dead cows, and now zits. I hate them all, but mostly I *hate that frog!*"

The next day the Pharaoh woke up, peeked over his blankets, looked out the window, and said just one word: *"Yikes!"* What he saw was ice balls falling from the sky. This was strange enough, because Egypt is a very warm country and it hardly ever snows there, much less has ice balls falling from the sky. But what was even more strange was that mixed in with the ice balls were balls of fire. When the fireballs hit people, the people screamed, "Ooch!" And when the ice balls hit them they yelled, "Ouch!" The Pharaoh just pulled the blankets over his head and covered his ears so he wouldn't hear the sounds of "Ooch! Ouch! Ooch! Ouch!" that were coming from all over Egypt.

While he was under the covers, he heard a frog voice. "Let's see now," the frog voice said. "Plague number one was blood, then there were frogs (that's how I got here), then fleas, then flies, then dead cows, then zits, and now we have the charming plague of ice balls with fire mixed in, and *still* you won't let the people go? What a dope!"

The next day, while the Pharaoh was eating his cereal, a bug flew into the Pharaoh's bowl. "Yuck, what was that?" he asked. Then he saw that the floor was filled with locusts. The frog was happily hopping around, gobbling some of them up. The frog smiled, burped, rubbed his fat tummy, and said, "I love the plagues I can eat! The fleas and flies were good, but these locusts are just delicious—keep it up, Einstein!"

"Who's Einstein?" asked the Pharaoh.

"Never mind," said the frog.

The next day the Pharaoh woke up at his usual time, but he looked outside and saw that it was still dark, so he went back to bed. He woke up again a little later, but it was still dark outside, so he went back to sleep again. Later on he sat up in bed, saw that it was still dark, and screamed, *"Where's the sun?* It's daytime, but there is no day! What's going on here?"

Then the Pharaoh went to the window and saw a really strange thing. Everywhere in Egypt it was dark…*except* over the houses of Moses and his people. Over their houses the sun was shining. This went on for three days, and by then all the Egyptians had gathered around the Israelite homes to tie their shoes, thread their needles, wash their clothes, and do everything that needed to be done in the daylight.

The Pharaoh was also going crazy from having no daytime. One day he put on some shepherd clothes, so nobody would recognize him, and joined the crowd in the sun around Moses' house. The people were talking about him. "That stupid Pharaoh. When is he going to learn that it's

wrong to have slaves, it's wrong to go against God, and it's wrong to wreck your country just because you're stubborn. Because of that dumb Pharaoh, our country has been filled with blood, frogs, fleas, flies, dead cows, zits, ice balls with fireballs mixed in, locusts, and now darkness in the daytime! It's just not fair!"

Then the Pharaoh, who was hiding in the crowd, threw off his robe and shouted, "I am the *Pharaoh*. I don't care what anybody thinks. I command the sun and the moon and the stars. Everyone and everything has to do what *I* say!"

Moses walked forward, looked the Pharaoh in the eye, and said, "Why don't you just command the sun to come out again?"

The Pharaoh squirmed and said, "I'm getting around to it."

Then Moses put his arm around the Pharaoh's shoulder and said to him quietly, "Listen to me, and listen well. This is the last time we will see each other. If you do not let my people go by this time tomorrow, the last plague will come, and it will be so horrible you will never forget it. Don't make God punish you and your people this way. You can't win. You can't stand against freedom, and you can't stand against God."

The Pharaoh said, "God has nothing to do with all this stuff. We are just having a run of bad luck, *real* bad luck! I am going home now and I am going to sleep. When I wake up, everything will be all right again. I will have good luck again. And one more thing, which I should have done at the beginning of all this. Moses, if you are in Egypt tomorrow, I will have my soldiers find you and kill you, along with that frog!"

But that's not what happened.

The next day the tenth plague happened. After the blood and after the frogs, after the fleas and after the flies, after the dead cows and after the zits, after the ice balls with the fireballs mixed in, after the locusts and after the darkness, every first-born person and animal died in all the land of Egypt. That day the Pharaoh cried a cry that was so loud that people all over Egypt heard him. That day the Pharaoh let the people go.

As Moses and his people walked out of Egypt with all their stuff and with all their animals, they did not cheer and they did not laugh and they did not sing. They saw how the plagues had ruined Egypt, and they were sad for the Egyptians, so they just left quietly.

The Pharaoh was alone. Between his tears he heard a frog way in the distance. The frog was croaking over and over, "You can't stand against freedom, and you can't stand against God!"

—*Exodus 7:14–12:36*

The Rock Words

The Rock
Words

....

When Moses got the Ten Commandments from God on the top of Mount Sinai, he wrote them down on the two big rocks. But Moses didn't write down *everything* God said. Moses knew that the more he wrote, the more rocks he would need, and the more rocks he would have to carry down the mountain. So Moses wrote short!

This is how it went with each commandment.

One

God spoke to Moses and said to him, "I am God. The first thing you are going to have to do is teach people what that means. I warn you, this is not going to be easy, because I am not like anything else. Some people may think I am some old man with a house in the clouds, but you know that's not true. Some people may think I have hands and feet and a big toe, but you know that's not true. Some people are going to want to see me before they will believe in me, but you know that can't happen, because I am invisible. So, some people will think that I am nowhere, but you know that I am everywhere. Explaining about me is going to be a tough job.

"Try to explain to the people that I made each one of them special. Explain to them that even though I made them good, I also made them free to be bad. I am strong, but I won't stop them from doing wrong. They have to learn to stop themselves. Some people may think that it's all right to do wrong because I won't stop them, but you better tell them that I will remember them and what they do, and I have a *terrific* memory. Explain to them that someday each and every one of them is going to die, and that is when their souls are going to have to have a little talk with me. Tell them that I love everybody just the way they are, but I also want everybody to keep trying to be better.

"Also remember, Moses, to explain to the people that I am the one they all have to thank for every good thing they ever get. Remind them that I am the one who took them out of Egypt so they could be free. I am the one who gave them such a good world to live in, and I am the one who made goofy animals like the platypus, so that they could have a good laugh."

Moses thought over what God had said to him and then carved these words into the rock:

I the Lord am your God who brought you out of the land of Egypt, the house of bondage, and gave you the platypus.

Then Moses thought some more and took out the part about the platypus.

Two

Then God spoke to Moses and said to him, "Tell people not to even *think* of having any other god. I made everything everywhere. I made everything in heaven. I made everything on earth. I made everything over, under, and *in* the water. I made everything that is sometimes under water but mostly on the land. I made everything that is sometimes on the land but mostly under water. I made everything that flies around, buzzes in your ear, and lands on your nose. I made everything fuzzy and cute. I made everything slimy and cold. I made everything with feathers and everything with scales. I made everything with bad breath and everything with sweet songs. *But* make sure you explain to the people that none of the things I made are me. None of them were made so that you would pray to them or love them like you love each other or like you love me. Teach the people that the whole universe is filled with just two kinds of things: stuff…and the one who made the stuff. I am the one who made the stuff.

"Now, I know that people want to worship what they can see, and they can't see me. I know they might pick out something they *can* see and call that thing God, but it isn't! Only *I* am God! People will worship mud if you let them, so be careful. It will take three or four generations for your kids to get it right if you get this wrong, but if you get it right, your children will get it right for a thousand generations.

"And if you get it wrong, and pray to some stuff that is not me, don't think for a minute that it does not matter, or that I am so big and so invisible that I don't really care and I will not be watching. I *do* care and I am *always* watching, and I will not be happy if you get it wrong, because…*I don't want people praying to stuff!* Anyway, remember, remember, remember…everything but me is not God."

Moses heard all this, thought it over, and carved this into the rock:

You shall not make for yourself a sculptured image, or any likeness of what is in the heavens above, or on the earth below, or in the waters under the earth. You shall not bow down to them or serve them. For I the Lord your God am an impassioned God, visiting the guilt of the parents upon the children, upon the third and upon the fourth generations of those who reject me, but showing kindness to the thousandth generation of those who love me and keep my commandments.

Three

Then God spoke to Moses and said to him, "Don't swear! People swear when something bad happens to them, so if they use my name when they swear, they will always think that I bring something bad. I don't want this. If you drop a rock on your foot, I am not the one who dropped it, so I should not get the blame. Get this straight: I am the place everything good comes from, so using my name to swear or curse is just not right.

"Now, I know you are thinking, If God is the place everything good comes from, then what is the place everything bad comes from? Good question, and here is the answer: Bad comes from two places—it comes from bad things you do even though I told you not to do bad things, and it also comes from holes in the world. I put holes in the world, like diseases, so that you can use the big brains I gave you to cure the diseases. I put the holes in the world so that you would have something important to do with your life on earth.

"So from now on, understand that my name should not be used with a curse word. My name should be used only with words that patch up the holes in the world or words that say *Thank you* or *I love you*. I know it's hard to control what you say if a rock falls on your foot, but try to say 'Ouch!' or 'Yeoow!' or 'Fudge!' or 'Framitz!' Don't you ever put my name and the word *damn* together. My name is a blessing. You know that. Everybody should know that."

Moses heard all this, thought about it, and shrank it down to these words he carved into the rock:

You shall not swear falsely by the name of the Lord your God: for the Lord will not clear one who swears falsely by God's name.

Four

Then God spoke to Moses and said to him, "Tell the people not to work all the time. Try to remember to rest at least one day out of seven, which is the day I call the sabbath. I call it sabbath because that word means *rest,* and resting is what that day is all about.

"You know what happens if you work all the time. If you work all the time, you will get old too fast, you will get tired too fast, you will get sick too fast! If you work all the time, you will not have enough time to spend with your children when they are growing up, and probably they will not want to spend time with you when you are growing old. If you work all the time, you will not notice the terrific things I put in the world for you to enjoy. Things like sunsets and butterflies, baseball, and hot fudge. Things like walking through crunchy leaves and dancing to music. Things like eating spaghetti or corn on the cob. Things like hugging and kissing or hiding and seeking.

"Working all the time also keeps you from sharing what you have with other folks, and helping people who need help, and teaching people who need to learn. Working all the time keeps you from doing the things that help you get outside yourself and really learn to feel the pain and the joy of others. What more do I have to say! Work will get you money, and money will get you things, but things will not fill up the empty place in your heart that comes from not having enough time to love somebody.

"I have given you only a few years to live on planet earth, and if you work all the time, those years will just slip away. That is why I have also given you the sabbath. To help you remember every week of every month of every year that work is not enough to fill up a life.

"By the way, resting on the sabbath day also gives you a very good time to gather together and pray together and say thank you to me for making the world, the world that gives you everything you need to live and be happy. After I made that world, I rested from making it. Now, if I rested, don't you think that you should rest, too?

"And one last thing. This resting is not just for you but also for any people who work for you. If you think that I want you to rest while everybody around you works, you have another think coming! All people are made in my image, and all people need rest, just like you. The same goes for the animals who work for you. They need rest, too. And

if there are strangers passing through your town, try to give them a place to rest and a good meal. They are probably lonely and wish they were home.

"So work hard and work well, and rest on the sabbath day and keep it special. You will be amazed at how terrific your life will be. Remember! Your work is just what you do, it's not what you are."

Moses heard all these words and shortened them down to this:

Remember the sabbath day and keep it holy. Six days you shall labor and do all your work, but the seventh day is a sabbath of the Lord your God: you shall not do any work—you, your son or daughter, your male or female slave, or your cattle, or the stranger who is within your settlements. For in six days the Lord made heaven and earth and sea, and all that is in them, and he rested on the seventh day; therefore the Lord blessed the sabbath day and hallowed it.

Five

Then God spoke to Moses and said to him, "Tell the children to do what their parents ask them to do, even if they think it's stupid. But you must also tell the children *not* to do what their parents ask them to do if it's wrong or if it hurts somebody. Tell the children that most of the things their parents ask them to do are good things, and right things, and things that will make them good people when they grow up. Tell the children that doing what their parents ask them to do is one of the big ways to show that they love and respect their parents.

"And tell the children that if they are going to do what their parents ask them to do, they should do it right away! Tell them they get no credit from me or from their parents for doing something after they have been asked to do it a hundred times. Children will learn soon enough that being a parent is hard. Babies don't come with instruction books on how to raise them. Most parents are just guessing most of the time, but most parents get it right, because when you love a child, most things kind of fall into place. I made love so that it works that way.

"Also tell the children that there may be times when their parents get old, and they will have to take care of them. This may be hard work for the children. It may cost money, and it may cost time, but remember that if one parent can take care of a whole bunch of children, then a whole bunch of children ought to be able to take care of one parent.

"Don't forget to teach the children that doing what their parents ask them to do right away is just one way to show love and respect. Doing things parents do *not* ask for and do *not* expect is sometimes even better than doing what they ask and what they want. Hugging and kissing your parents for no special reason, thanking them for going shopping for food, telling them you are proud of them and that you think they did a good job raising you, letting them win at a game you are better at, asking for their advice whenever you can and even taking that advice sometimes, calling on them just to see if they are well—all these are terrific ways to honor your parents that go way beyond picking up your socks and making your bed.

"Maybe the best way to show you love and respect your parents is to raise good children of your own. That way your parents can see that you really did grow up okay because of them. That's the whole thing! Moses, you must teach children the most important thing they need to know about their parents is that *they are because of them*. Teach the children never to forget that they are alive because of their parents, that they know what is right because of their parents, and that they have hope, courage, and strength because of their parents. That's the whole thing children need to learn about parents: *They are because of them*."

Moses heard all this, but he didn't have enough rocks to write it all down, so he just wrote:

Honor your father and your mother, that you may long endure on the land that the Lord your God is assigning to you.

Six

Then God spoke to Moses and said to him, "Life is so special, everybody must learn that I am the only one who can give it, and I am the only one who can take it away. Because life is the best thing, murder is the worst thing. Murder not only kills a person, it also kills everybody who might come from that person. Murder also kills a part of the lives of the people who loved the person who was murdered. Murder is the most terrible thing a person can do. That's how bad it is.

"Now, not all killing is murder. If you have to kill a person to save your own life, that is sad, but it is not bad. If you have to fight in a war to keep some enemy from taking over your country, that is also sad, but it is also not bad. But killing people is a *very* big thing, and if you kill another person to save your life, you better be sure that you had *no other choice*! And if you go to war to defend your country, you better be sure that your country is really being attacked! Killing people is a big thing, but sometimes it is a big thing you just have to do. Most of the time it is a big thing that you had better never do, or you will be in big trouble with me.

"In fact, everything that is alive should be left alive unless you need to kill it to eat it for food or unless you have to kill it to keep it from killing you. I am the giver and taker of life, and I put you on the earth to protect life, not destroy it! Remember that *everybody* and *everything* has a right to live. That right to live comes from me, and you can't take it away. Not now. Not ever."

Moses heard all this, and he thought it over, and he did a *real* good job of shortening what God said to him down to just these words:

You shall not murder.

Seven

Then God spoke to Moses and said to him, "Getting married is a special holy thing to do. Doing it means that you want to live the rest of your life with only *that* person as your husband or your wife. Being married means that you sleep with only one person, and that person is your husband or your wife. So remember, it's okay to sleep with a teddy bear, and it's okay to sleep with a fuzzy duck, and it's okay to sleep with a stuffed bunny, but it is *not* okay to sleep with somebody who is married to somebody else."

Moses was married, and he knew about this already, and so he just chiseled these words into the rock:

You shall not commit adultery.

Eight

Then God spoke to Moses and said to him, "Teach the people that stealing is bad. Stealing is bad because it's just not fair to take somebody else's stuff. You have no right to take stuff. You have a right only to earn stuff. Most people know this already, but stealing is still going to be a big problem, because there are so many kinds of stealing.

"If you get some extra change at the store and don't give it back, that's stealing. If you are selling something, and you say it is good when you know it's really just junk, that's also stealing. If you copy from your neighbor's test paper, that's stealing. If you take somebody else's idea and say that it's your idea, that's stealing, too. There are lots of ways to steal, but there is only one way to be honest. So don't take anything that isn't yours, and give back what you get by mistake, and don't make people think that something is true when it is not true. If you do this, you will be just fine.

"But no matter how carefully you guard your stuff, somehow, someway, somebody is going to find a way to steal some of your stuff during your life. When this happens, don't get so angry that you decide to start stealing from somebody else. Stealing makes you as bad as the person who stole from you. Trust me. Don't become a thief. Remember, I will make things right some day."

Moses heard all this and knew that people would get the idea if he just wrote:

You shall not steal.

Nine

Then God spoke to Moses and said to him, "Tell the truth! If you lie, nobody will trust you. If you lie, you will forget the difference between what's true and what isn't. And if you lie, judges won't be able to decide fairly who to put in jail and who to let go free. The best reason to tell the truth is that I say so, and I would not say so if it was not the right thing to do.

"Now, Moses, you must teach the people that *sometimes* it is okay to tell a little lie. If somebody who did nothing wrong is hiding from a bully in your house, and the bully comes around and asks if that person is in your house because they want to beat up that person, then you *should* lie and say that the person is not in your house, because protecting somebody who didn't do anything wrong is more important than telling the truth to a bully.

"Also, if your friend is wearing some new clothes that he or she really likes and worked hard to buy, but you think that the clothes look goofy, and your friend asks you what you think, it may be a good idea to lie and tell them that you like the clothes, because telling them the truth would hurt their feelings.

"Also, if two of your friends are fighting and a little lie will help them make up and be friends again, then that little lie is also okay with me. I do not mind lies like these, but be careful! Lying is a dangerous habit to get into, even if you are lying to make people feel better or to protect somebody.

"Knowing when to lie and when to tell the truth is one of the real hard things in life. I wish I could help you know what to do all the time, but I can't. You just have to learn how to do the right thing. Learning makes you grow up. The point is that telling the truth is *almost* always the best thing to do, but not *always, always.*"

Moses heard all this and knew that it was true, but he also didn't want to have ten rocks with only one long commandment on each of them, so he just chiseled:

You shall not bear false witness against your neighbor.

Ten

Then God spoke to Moses and said to him, "Tell people not to want what their neighbors have, especially if what they want is their neighbor's stuff. I am not against stuff, but there are more important things in the world than stuff.

"If your neighbor is a nice person, it is good to want to be a nice person like your neighbor. If your neighbor is a brave person, it is good to want to be brave like your neighbor. But don't want your neighbor's stuff, because stuff will not make you a better person. That is what these ten commandments are all about. They are about making you a better person, not just a person with better stuff."

Moses heard all this, but he was coming to the end of the second rock, and he knew he could not lift any more than two rocks at the most, so he just finished up the Ten Commandments by writing these words:

You shall not covet your neighbor's house: you shall not covet your neighbor's wife, or his male or female slave, or his ox or his ass, or anything that is your neighbor's.

And after Moses had finished writing down all these rock words, God came to Moses and said, "You shortened them up just right. Thanks."

And Moses said to God, "You're welcome. Now could you help me lift these rocks?"

When Moses brought the rock words down to the people, even the short way Moses wrote them down was not short enough. They wanted a *really* short version of the Ten Commandments that would fit on one medium-sized stone, not two big rocks. So Moses wrote down this extra-short copy of the rock words for people who could not read a lot of words or for people who traveled a lot and did not want to pack a lot of rocks:

1. *There's just one God.*
2. *Don't even think of having another God.*
3. *Don't curse with God's name.*
4. *Rest one day out of seven.*
5. *Do what your mom and dad tell you to do, and do it right away (unless what they tell you to do is really bad).*
6. *Don't kill anyone who is not trying to kill you.*
7. *Make love only to the person you marry.*
8. *Don't take stuff that isn't yours.*
9. *Tell the truth (almost always).*
10. *Don't want what other people have just because they have it.*

—*Exodus 20:1–14*

The Commandments
on Moses' Sleeves

....

Moses thought that after the tenth commandment, God was finished, but he was wrong. After giving Moses the tenth commandment,
God went right on and gave Moses commandment number eleven.
Moses didn't know what to do. He had already filled up two big rocks
with the first ten commandments, and he knew that there was no way
he could lift *three* rocks. Moses wasn't even sure he could lift two! But
Moses didn't want to tell God to stop, so he just kept on writing down
the extra commandments on his sleeves. Moses figured that after he got
down the mountain, he would copy them off his sleeves and carve them
onto new rocks.

Here are the commandments Moses wrote on his sleeves:

Eleven

God spoke to Moses and said to him, "You may think cutting a line
is a little thing, but it is really a big thing. When people are waiting in
line for something and you sneak into line ahead of them, what you are
really saying to all the people in the line is something like, 'The rules in
life are for you but not for me. I get to do what I want whenever I want
to do it, and without waiting, because I am more important than all of
you jerks! I don't care how long you have been waiting in this line
because I don't care about you!'

"Sneaking into line is one of the many bad things we do that we
think are little because they are not like robbing a bank or shooting

somebody. But Moses, you need to teach the people this big thing: *The way people get bad in big ways is that they get bad in little ways first. The way people end up doing big bad things that matter is by first doing little bad things and thinking that they don't matter.*

"You can also tell them, Moses, that when they die and their souls go to heaven, I have a big long line up here that goes *nowhere,* and all the people who sneaked into line here on earth get to wait in that line for a *very* long time."

Even though Moses was only writing on his sleeves, not on rocks, Moses had a good idea that he might run out of sleeves, so he just wrote:

Don't cut a line.

Twelve

God spoke to Moses and said to him, "Not saying *please* when you want something and not saying *thank you* when you get something is another little bad thing that makes big bad things happen.

"*Please* and *thank you* are not the most important words: *I love you* is much more important. But *please* and *thank you* are right up there. *Please* and *thank you* are words that start you out being thankful and grateful for what you have and for what you get. Some people get spoiled and selfish just by forgetting to say *please* and *thank you* for what they want and for what they get.

"*Please* and *thank you* are kind of like a selfish thermometer. If you are worried about your children turning into spoiled brats, just write down how many times they say *please* and *thank you.* If they never say these words, they are spoiled for sure, and if they always say them, they are safe from being spoiled for sure. If they say them sometimes, they could go either way, and you should talk to them and remind them that *please* and *thank you* are the 'magic' words. They are magic because they open up your heart and they let other people in. *Please* and *thank you* also remind you that you can't get through life without a lot of help. And if you expect that help to keep coming, you better keep the *pleases* and the *thank yous* coming. These are the words that give people the biggest push in the direction of being nice.

"And one last thing, Moses. Please tell everybody thank you from me. I know it is hard to be a person on planet earth, but most people are doing a great job, and I am more proud of them than they will ever know. Well, come to think of it, they will all know just how proud I am of them someday."

Moses knew that all he really had to write down was this:

Always say please *and* thank you.

Thirteen

God spoke to Moses and said to him, "If you look both ways before you cross the street, there is much more of a chance that you will cross safely than if you just run out there into the street and hope for the best. That is the main reason to look both ways. In fact, the way some folks drive, it might be a good idea to look both ways before you walk on the sidewalk!

"Looking both ways before you cross the street has other good things to say for it. You just might get the idea to look both ways before you cross *anything*! Looking both ways helps you see things coming from another direction. Sometimes you only get ready for things to happen one way, and then—*wham*—they happen another way. It's good to be ready for things that come in ways you did not expect. That's what looking both ways really means. Also, looking both ways helps you to think about what will happen next.

"People do lots of goofy and stupid things and get hurt because they just don't think about what will happen next. So before you start to smoke, before you start to drink, before you do drugs, before you jump off a bridge with just rubber bands attached to your feet, before you do anything that looks like fun from just one direction, make sure you look in the other direction, too. Looking both ways is good advice for crossing streets, but it is even better advice for crossing life."

Moses was running out of sleeves, so he wrote:

Look both ways before you cross the street.

Fourteen

God spoke to Moses and said to him, "People say too many bad things about other people, and that's the truth. If you have nothing nice to say—nothing that will make somebody else feel happier or prettier or luckier, nothing that will help and not hurt, nothing that will lift up and not tear down—then my advice is to just shut up! Life is hard enough without other people dumping on you. You know that, so don't be the dumper unless you are ready to be the dumpee. Remember that nobody gets a good name by dragging other people's names through the mud.

"Now, Moses, you must teach the people that sometimes they will have to say things that are not nice. If they see a friend getting into trouble, they must say something to try and stop their friend before it is too late. Really, the things you say to a friend who is about to mess up his or her life *are* nice things, even if they don't sound nice to the person who hears them. Nice things can be hard things to hear and still be nice.

"If you try to say something nice whenever you speak, you will be surprised at just how many nice things you can find to say about other people. The amazing thing is this: The more nice things you say, the more nice things you will see."

Moses wrote on one of the last clean edges of his sleeve:

If you can't say anything nice, don't say anything at all.

Fifteen

God spoke to Moses and said to him, "Some folks have too much stuff, and some folks do not have enough stuff. That is one of the worst things you will learn about the world. There are lots of reasons for this, and sometimes there is not a lot you can do about it. One of the things you *can* do about the bad way stuff gets divided up on earth is to always try to share your stuff.

"Learning to share your stuff with friends is easy, because sharing with people you love is easy. The harder thing, and the thing I want you to try to teach people to do, is for people to share their stuff with people they don't even know: people who need it but are too ashamed to ask; people who need it but are too sick to ask; people who need it but are too far away to ask; people who need it but don't know the address or telephone number and can't write or call to ask, 'Could you please share your stuff with me?'

"Sharing your stuff makes your soul bigger and your life better, and it keeps you from becoming a selfish pig. Sharing your stuff is the best medicine for the disease of selfishness. It cures it every time!"

By this time, Moses was beginning to look for places to write on his pants, but he found a little more room at the end of his left sleeve and wrote:

Share your stuff.

Sixteen

God spoke to Moses and said to him, "Nobody wants to take out the garbage. The bag could break and spill chicken bones and old soup cans all over the sidewalk, and then you have to clean it all up. People just hate to take out the garbage, but somebody has to do it, so it might as well be you. You see, Moses, taking out the garbage is like lots of other dirty work nobody likes to do—taking out the garbage teaches a big lesson about life. Life is not all roses, and anyway, roses end up becoming part of the garbage, too.

"So teach the people to get used to doing some hard, dirty work in their lives. If all the work you do is clean and neat and easy, and if nothing smells about the work, you may start looking down on people who have to do dirty work every day of their lives. That is wrong. They are as good as you, as holy as you. So you should do some dirty work now and again to remind yourself about all the kinds of work that needs to get done if you are going to live together in peace on planet earth and not drown in your own garbage."

Moses was out of sleeves after he wrote this:

Take out the garbage.

Moses' sleeves were covered with commandments eleven through sixteen when he came down the mountain with the two big rocks that had commandments one through ten on them. He walked home, put the rocks down, took off his clothes, and fell asleep on his bed for about two days. While Moses was sleeping, his wife, Zipporah, washed his clothes, and when Moses woke up, he was glad to have clean clothes for about a second. That's how long it took for Moses to realize that the extra commandments had been washed away.

After thinking for a while, Moses remembered the extra commandments, but as he took his hammer and chisel and went to find some new, clean rocks, a bunch of his friends stopped him and said, "Moses, you have been up on the mountain too long! Ten of these commandments are hard enough! Most of us can't do more than six, and we're your friends! We know lots of folks who won't even be able to do two! Don't even think of writing down more commandments!"

Moses sort of agreed, but he did tell his friends and a few other people the extra commandments he had written down on his sleeves. These folks told their children, and over the years the extra commandments got passed down from parents to children, who then told them to their children when they became parents. So if you want to hear commandments one through ten, listen to the Bible. But if you want to hear commandments eleven through sixteen, listen to your parents!

—*Exodus 20:1, 24:3–4*

Gluing the Broken
Commandments Back Together

······································

Moses was always a go-fast person. Moses ran to school. Moses ran to the playground. Moses ran to lunch. Moses just wanted to get everywhere fast and get everywhere first. God liked Moses, but God did want to slow Moses down just a little.

When Moses took the children of Israel and a whole bunch of other people out of Egypt, Moses was the first one to run right out of Egypt. He was at the front of the crowd with all the other go-fast people—the teenagers and the joggers. The problem was that leaving Egypt was not a go-fast kind of thing. Leaving Egypt was kind of like driving to Florida with your family. Somebody always wanted to stop to go to the bathroom. Somebody was always hungry. Somebody was always crying, and somebody was always fighting with his or her sister.

Another thing that slowed down the people leaving Egypt was the people who could *never* go fast. There were folks leaving Egypt who had no legs, or one leg, or broken legs and who had to limp along or be carried or ride in a wagon. There were old people who had to keep stopping to catch their breath, wipe their foreheads, and say, "Oh, boy, it's hot!" There were blind people who needed guide dogs. There were short people who could not see over the tops of the sand dunes and tall people who kept getting blown over by the wind. There were even people who were so scared of everything they never wanted to move. This was not a go-fast group!

Moses would complain to God, "There are too many broken people here." God would try to explain to Moses that each person was special and each person was moving as fast as he or she could move. God tried to slow Moses down by setting up a pillar of smoke in the daytime and a pillar of fire at night. When the smoke or fire moved, God let the people move. When it stopped, God made the people stop. Both the fire and the smoke did not move fast at all.

Slowly, slowly, the people and the smoke and the fire and Moses got to Mount Sinai. God told Moses to climb up the mountain and get the Ten Commandments. Of course Moses climbed Mount Sinai real fast, so to slow Moses down, God made Moses wait forty days and forty nights before giving him the Ten Commandments.

By the time Moses came down the mountain, the people had made a golden statue of a little cow and were dancing around it singing, "Moses is gone! His time is past! Tomorrow we'll all go real fast!" Moses was so angry at the people for making the cow statue their god that he smashed the Ten Commandments into a thousand pieces.

Then Moses went back up the mountain to get a new set of commandments from God. But God said to Moses, "What are you, nuts? I just gave you the best thing I could, and you smashed it because you were angry at a cow! It wasn't even a real cow! It was just a statue of a cow. Why should I give you another copy? If I give you another set of the commandments, you will probably just get angry again and smash them, too. Forget it, Moses! You had 'em, you smashed 'em, you glue 'em back together."

Moses said, "God, there's no way I can put the Ten Commandments back together. I smashed them into a thousand pieces."

God said, "Then get a thousand people to pick them up!"

"God, I don't have any rock glue!" Moses cried, but God wasn't listening.

Moses went down the mountain and said, "God told me to put the pieces of the commandments back together again. Who will help me?"

The go-fast people said to Moses, "These are just broken pieces of rock. Forget it, Moses. We're out of here." So Moses went back to the place where he smashed the Ten Commandments and started to look through the rocks. He found a couple of pieces with whole words, and some pieces with a couple of letters, and some pieces with just a piece of a letter. By nightfall, Moses had a pile of words and letters, but he had no way to fit them together. He fell asleep, crying.

In the morning, Moses woke up to an amazing sight. All around him were people looking for pieces of the Ten Commandments. There were folks with no legs, or one leg, or broken legs crawling around on the ground. There were old people who would find a few pieces, stop to catch their breath, wipe their foreheads, and say, "Oh, boy, it's hot!" There were blind people who were feeling around for the rocks with writing on them. There were *also* some of the go-fast people who thought about things a little and decided that going fast was okay unless you missed everything that was going on around you. All these people were out there helping Moses in the place where he smashed the commandments.

By the end of the day the pile of pieces with words and letters and pieces of letters was much bigger, but after a week of trying to put the pieces together, they had only put together about half of the commandments, and some of the people were starting to give up. Moses said to them, "Don't worry how long it takes. The Ten Commandments are the best thing God ever gave us. I broke them because of your cow and because of my anger. We have to go slowly and fix what we messed up."

It was then that God told Moses to come back up the mountain and get another copy of the Ten Commandments. When Moses came down the mountain this time, there was no golden cow, just the people waiting for Moses and hoping he was all right.

God told Moses to make a special golden decorated box to hold the Ten Commandments so that they would not get smashed by accident. It took a long time to make the box, but nobody complained and nobody wanted to go fast.

When it was all done, Moses put the commandments in the box, and

then he said to the people, "I know that we should put the broken pieces into the box with the whole commandments. I know now that we should remember that even the broken pieces of God's words are holy. And most of all I know now that nobody is a broken person because of their age or their hearing or because of their sight or their speed or their memory. I'm sorry. I should have known that all along. Thanks to all of you who taught me that really the only broken people are the people who lose hope or who forget that God is with them and loves them always."

So they put the whole copy of the Ten Commandments and the smashed-up pieces of the Ten Commandments into the same golden decorated box. And they carried it in the middle of the line of people every single day. And nobody complained that carrying the box made them go slower. From that day on Moses walked at the back of the line of people, helping the people with one leg to limp along, and helping the people who were blind find a dog to guide them. To the old people who had stopped along the way to catch their breath and wipe their foreheads, Moses would say, "Oh, boy, it's hot!"

And they would say to him, "You ain't kidding, sonny—but don't worry. We're all going to get to where God wants us to go…just as long as we don't go too fast."

—Exodus 32:1–19, 34:1–2

God's
Mailbox

Bless Me, Too!

....

Blessings are funny things. Nowadays the only time you hear the word *bless* is when somebody near you sneezes and folks say, "God bless you!"…and what they are really thinking is God, I hope none of those sneeze germs got on me! Well, in the old days, the days of Abraham, Isaac and Jacob, Sarah, Rebekah, Leah, and Rachel, people were much more serious about blessings. In the old days, a blessing was a big-time, one-time thing, and it had nothing to do with sneezing. When a father was old and about to die, he would give a blessing to his son. That blessing was called the Big Last Blessing. Mostly, the Big Last Blessing went to the oldest son, but not always. The big thing about the Big Last Blessing was that once the old, dying father gave it to one of his sons, he could not ever take it back or change it!

Every son wanted to get the Big Last Blessing because of what came with it. If you got the Big Last Blessing, you got all your father's stuff, and you got to be the head of the family and the boss of everybody else, and if you didn't get the Big Last Blessing, you got nothing.

Abraham had two sons: Isaac and Ishmael. Only one could get the Big Last Blessing, and even though Abraham said he loved them both the same, he really loved Isaac more. Isaac was the son of Sarah, who was Abraham's favorite wife. Whenever they were playing and got into a fight, no matter whose fault it was, Abraham would say, "Ishmael! Why are you picking on your brother Isaac? Let him alone!" Just before Abraham died, he gave Isaac the Big Last Blessing.

Ishmael cried and said, "Daddy, bless me, too!" but once the Big Last

Blessing was given out, there was nothing for anybody else.

Isaac had two sons: Jacob and Esau. Isaac didn't even pretend he loved them both. He said in front of everybody in the family, "I love Esau more than Jacob, because Esau is a hunter and Jacob is a wimp!"

Jacob knew from the time he was little that Esau was going to get the Big Last Blessing. He went to Isaac and cried, "Daddy, bless me, too!" But Isaac didn't listen to Jacob.

Just before Isaac died, when he was very old and very blind, he asked Esau to make him some special stew, and then he would give Esau the Big Last Blessing. Isaac's wife, Rebekah, heard this, and since she loved Jacob more than Esau, while Esau was out in the fields hunting for the wild animal that would be the meat in the stew, she and Jacob made up another pot of stew and tricked Isaac into giving the Big Last Blessing to Jacob. When Esau came back with the stew for his father, Isaac realized that he had blessed the wrong kid, but it was too late to do anything about it, because, remember, you just can't change a Big Last Blessing. Esau cried, "Daddy, bless me, too!" But Isaac could not listen to Esau.

Jacob grew up and had twelve sons and a daughter. Thirteen children was a big family, even in those days, but all the children did not come from just one mother. That's because husbands were allowed to have more than one wife back then. Jacob had four wives: Rachel, Leah, Bilhah, and Zilpah.

One of Jacob's sons was named Joseph. He was the son of Rachel, who was Jacob's favorite wife, and so all the other brothers thought that Joseph would be the one to get the Big Last Blessing. One day Jacob gave Joseph a beautiful coat of many colors. That did it. The brothers got together and planned to get rid of Joseph, saying, "Dad can't bless that little creep if he can't find him!" And so, when they got the chance, they sold their brother Joseph as a slave to some people going to Egypt. They dipped his coat of many colors into some sheep blood and told Jacob that Joseph had been killed by a wild animal.

When Jacob saw the bloody coat and heard the story, he knew that

his sons were lying. Jacob knew that if a wild animal had wanted to eat one of his sons, it would have picked out a fat, slow son like Reuben or Levi, and not a fast, skinny son like Joseph. Jacob knew right away that his sons had done something bad to Joseph to keep Joseph from getting the Big Last Blessing.

Joseph went down to Egypt as a slave, but he didn't stay a slave for very long. God helped him get good at figuring out dreams for people, and figuring out dreams has always been a good job. One day the Pharaoh needed to figure out a dream, so he called on Joseph, who did such a good job of figuring out the Pharaoh's dream that the Pharaoh made Joseph free and rich.

When the rains stopped falling in the land of Israel, Joseph's brothers went down to Egypt to buy food, and that's where they found Joseph and Joseph found them. They all said they were sorry, and they all meant it.

When Jacob was very old and felt sure that his time to die was coming close, he called all his children together, and he told them that it was time for the Big Last Blessing. All the children of Jacob screamed, "Oh, no! Not the Big Last Blessing! Do anything, Father, but please don't do the Big Last Blessing! We *hate* the Big Last Blessing!"

Jacob said, "Don't worry, my children. The Big Last Blessing is over. It is over because the Big Last Blessing was a bad idea. The Big Last Blessing made one child rich and everybody else miserable. That's bad. The Big Last Blessing was never given by a mother and never given to a girl. That's terrible. God never even asked anyone to give a Big Last Blessing. I don't know how it all got started, but I do know how it is all going to end. It's going to end with me. I am going to bless each one of my children with a blessing that is just for you, and I am going to let you share all my stuff when I die. None of you will get more, and none of you will get less."

All the children of Jacob cheered and hugged their father. Jacob called each of his children to him and gave each of them a little blessing and a big hug. Then he said, "I love you all, just the same, just as much, just as strong, just as deep. Each of you is a blessing to me. Now go out and be a blessing to the world."

And then Jacob died, and everybody around agreed that his life had been the biggest blessing of all.

—*Genesis 27:34*

Cutting
Corners

....

Korah was always worried about people taking his stuff. When he was a kid and other kids came over to play rocks, which was the only game back then, he would always count his rocks when the kids left to see if anybody had stolen one of them. When Korah grew up, he never changed. When he grew grapes, he counted every grape. When he grew wheat, he counted every stalk. It was such a silly sight to see a big wheat field with little name tags on every stalk of wheat, or a big vineyard with numbers written on every grape. Everybody who saw it said the same thing: "That's just stupid, selfish old Korah doing something stupid and selfish again to make sure that nobody takes his stuff." Moses was a relative of Korah's and tried to get him to change, but even Moses had no luck.

When the wheat was all grown, Korah cut it stalk by stalk and picked up every grain that fell to the ground. Moses said to Korah, "You can't do that. God told us to leave the wheat we drop in the fields, so poor people can come into the fields when we are done and pick up the dropped wheat and make bread for themselves, too."

"Let the poor people get dropped wheat from some other guy's field!" growled Korah. "Nobody takes my stuff!"

When Korah cut the wheat stalks, he cut every stalk in every field, all the way to the corners. Moses said to Korah, "You can't do that. God told us not to cut the corners of our fields, so poor people can come in and cut the wheat that is growing in the corners and make bread for themselves, too."

"Let them get wheat from the corners of some other guy's field," kvetched Korah. "Nobody takes my stuff!"

When Korah picked the grapes from his grapevines, he picked every single grape, counting each one as he put it into a basket. Moses told Korah, "You can't do that. God told us to leave some grapes on the vine, so poor people can come into our vineyards and pick some leftover grapes and make some wine for themselves, too."

"Let them pick the leftover grapes from some other guy's vineyard," snickered Korah. "Nobody takes my stuff!" Korah painted a big sign and put it in his wheat field. The sign read: WHEAT WHACKERS STAY AWAY! He put a sign in his vineyard that read: GRAPE GRABBERS GET LOST!

That is how things went for years. Korah got selfisher and selfisher and richer and richer. Then one year something really weird happened. That year brought a great harvest of wheat and grapes for everybody except Korah. When rain fell, it fell on everybody's fields except Korah's. When the sun came out, it shone on everybody's fields except Korah's. When the bugs came, they skipped over everybody else's fields and ate up everything in Korah's. By the end of the growing time, everybody had big crops except Korah, who had no crops. All Korah had was lots and lots of dust and bugs.

Korah had used up all his money buying bug killers and getting water, but nothing helped. Korah had no food in his house, he had no wine, no grapes, no apples, no honey, and no bread. Lots of people were happy that Korah had nothing. Most folks were saying behind his back, "That good-for-nothing selfish pig Korah! I hope he learns now what it's like to have nothing." Korah just sat there in his dusty, buggy fields with his head in his hands, crying.

Korah would have starved if it were not for Moses. Moses brought him bread and grapes, and tried to cheer him up. Then harvesttime came along, and Moses took Korah with him. "Where are we going?" Korah asked Moses.

"Just come along and you will see."

They went to a field nearby that had been harvested already, but the corners of the field still had wheat stalks growing and there was lots of cut wheat lying on the ground. A whole bunch of poor people were standing around the field, waiting.

Just then the farmer said, "Okay, come on in, everybody. The stuff in this field is for anybody who needs it. I did not cut the corners, and I didn't pick up anything that fell to the ground, so there's plenty here for all of you." The poor people ran into the field, but Korah just stood there.

"It's not my field," Korah said to Moses. "It's not my wheat. I can't take it. I would rather starve."

Moses put his arm around Korah and spoke softly to him. "Korah, everything is God's. The wheat and the grapes, the farmer and the fields, the sun and the rain, the bugs and the cows—everything is God's. We are just kind of renting all this stuff from God, and we show that we know God owns everything by giving away some of what God gives to us. It's really simple. God owns everything, and we don't need to take it all."

Korah tried to smile; he said, "All I have to give away is bugs."

Then a little girl came over to Korah, handed him a few stalks of wheat, and said, "Here, mister. God gave us enough. You take some."

That night Korah ate bread and grapes. After he ate, he prayed to God. This was the first prayer he ever prayed to God: "God, thank you for sharing your stuff with me. I will try to share my stuff from now on."

The next year Korah's fields got sun and rain, and the wheat grew tall, and the grapes grew plump and juicy. At harvesttime, Korah called everybody to his fields and said, "This year I did not cut the corners of my field. In fact, this year I did not cut anything. I am giving all my wheat and all my grapes to the people who got nothing from me for so many years. And if there is anything left over, I will leave it for the wild animals." Everybody cheered Korah, and Moses gave him a big hug.

That night even the bunnies had bread and grapes to eat. That night everybody had enough stuff.

—Leviticus 19:9

Three Green Things
and a Yellow

....

One day God was talking to Moses about the future. God told Moses that even though all the people Moses knew lived in tents and herded sheep, in the future hardly anyone would live in tents or herd sheep. "How will they live, and what will they do all day?" Moses asked God with great interest.

"In the future," God answered Moses, "people will live in houses and apartments, and they will use computers to do their work."

"What's a house?" Moses asked.

God thought and said, "A house is like a stiff tent that stays in one place all the time."

"What's an apartment?" Moses asked.

God answered, "An apartment is like a bunch of houses stacked on top of each other to save space."

"Will there be no space in the future?" Moses asked.

God said, "There will be plenty of space, but not in the cities, where most of the people want to live. That's why they will need apartments."

Moses said, "I don't understand. Why will people want to live in the cities, where they have to stack up their houses, when there is plenty of space in the hills and fields?"

God said, "That's a very good question, Moses. I don't quite understand it myself. As near as I can figure it, people will want to live in the cities because the cities will have most of the good jobs and all of the good restaurants."

"What's a restaurant?" Moses asked.

God answered, "A restaurant is a place where other people cook you all sorts of wonderful kinds of food, and when you are done eating, they clean up everything. You pay them some money to do this for you."

"I wish we had restaurants now," Moses said, sighing.

"Don't worry," God said. "You will have them soon enough."

Moses asked, "Will there be trees in the cities?"

God answered, "Not enough. There will not be nearly enough trees in the cities, and the air will be so bad in most cities that the trees that are there will have a tough time growing."

"Maybe the people in the future will find a way to keep the good restaurants and get rid of the bad air?" Moses asked.

"Maybe," God answered.

After a pause, Moses asked, "What's a computer?"

"A computer," God answered, "counts things and writes things down very fast."

"Why will the people in the future need to count and write so fast? Will they have that many sheep to count?" Moses asked.

"No," said God. "Most of them will have no sheep. Most of them will live by doing things that have nothing to do with animals or with the land, but the things they will do for a living will be things that need fast counting and fast writing, and that is why they will need computers."

Moses asked God, "Isn't there any way for you to help people remember the land and tents and sheep even when they are living in cities, eating in restaurants, and counting and writing on computers?"

God thought for a time and then said, "I have an idea to help people remember the land. I will give them a holiday where they have to sleep outside in booths. That way at least once a year they will remember what the dew smells like on the growing things at night and what the stars look like when they are lying down and looking up at night."

Moses thought and said, "What's a booth?"

God answered quickly, "The kind of booth I have in mind will be sort of like a tent with a top that is made of leafy green things instead of animal skins."

"I like your plan," said Moses. "It will definitely smell better than a tent made of animal skins. What are they going to put in the booths to remember the land?"

God told Moses. "I am going to have them bring fruit and gourds and pumpkins and cornstalks and apples and honey and maybe some peanut butter and jelly sandwiches into the booths."

"They are going to love the sandwiches," Moses said, even though he had never tasted peanut butter and jelly. He figured it was some kind of fancy restaurant food.

God said, "That's not all, Moses. I am going to ask them to bring into the booths on this holiday three green things and a yellow."

Moses said, "What?"

And God said, "I have picked out three green things and one yellow thing that will remind the city people of the land and the things that grow on it."

"What's the yellow thing?" Moses asked.

God said, "It's a citron."

"What's a citron?"

God answered, "A citron is kind of like a wrinkled-up lemon with no juice."

Moses laughed. "Why in the world would you pick such a goofy fruit?"

God answered, "Because the citron smells great when you scratch it, and that will teach people that you have to scratch the world before it smells good. It will teach them that they have to find the beauty of the world by going out and scratching around, not just by reading about it or watching it on television."

"What's television?" Moses asked.

"I'll tell you later," God answered. "It comes after restaurants and before computers."

Moses asked, "What are the green things you want people to bring into the booths along with the goofy juiceless lemon?"

God said, "I want them to bring a palm frond."

"What's a frond?"

"A frond is a palm leaf," God answered.

"Then why don't they call it a leaf?"

"They don't call it a leaf because it's a frond!"

"Oh," Moses said. "What's the palm *frond* supposed to teach them?"

"The palm frond," God said, "stands up straight and tall, and that will teach them to stand up tall and fight for the earth."

"What are the other two green things?"

"A branch from the myrtle tree and a branch from the weeping willow tree."

"What in the world are they for?" Moses asked.

God said, "Each leaf from the myrtle tree is shaped like an eye, and this will teach them to keep a close eye out for anybody who is throwing junk into my clean air and water and land. The weeping willow branch is to teach them—"

"I know what!" Moses said, interrupting. "The weeping willow will remind people to cry for all the animals we kill, or who lose their homes when we cut down the trees they live in, or who get sick from the junk we spill into the water, the air, and the land. If we don't care, we can't cry, and if we can't cry, we can't get angry enough to change things so that the world you gave us stays clean. Is that what the weeping willow is supposed to teach us?"

"That's exactly it," God said softly. "Three greens and a yellow, for a world that came to you clean and needs all of you to help keep it clean."

"Now can you tell me about television?" Moses asked God.

"Later," God said. "Go read a book."

—*Leviticus 23:39–43*

Elisha the
Pancake Hunter

....

People like eggs, and the main reason is pancakes. If you don't have eggs, you can't make pancakes, and if you don't have pancakes, you have to eat oatmeal for breakfast every morning. Now, oatmeal is good for you, but in a choice between oatmeal and pancakes, most folks will go for the pancakes every time. So the point here is simple: People need pancakes, and pancakes need eggs, so people need eggs.

In the old days, people got eggs in different ways. Some folks put egg cartons out in the woods at night where the wild chickens lived and hoped that by the morning the chickens would lay a few eggs in the cartons. This was a goofy idea even back then. Mostly when folks wanted pancakes, they would go out and hire a pancake hunter. The pancake hunter was a person who would sneak around the forest looking for birds' nests, because where there were birds' nests, there were sure to be eggs, and where there were eggs, there were going to be pancakes!

If the pancake hunters found a nest with eggs, but the mother bird was still sitting on the nest, they would sneak up on the nest and by shouting "Booga booga!" scare the mother bird away so she wouldn't peck at them while they were taking her eggs. Then they would bring the eggs back to the person who hired them. The person would get pancakes, and the hunter would get cash (and usually a pancake or two for his troubles).

Then one day a very good pancake hunter named Elisha thought to himself, Why should I let the mother bird go? If I take her *and* the eggs, I will have *two* things to sell. And so it was. From that day on, the pan-

cake hunters took both the mother bird to sell for mother-bird soup and the eggs to sell for pancakes. They did this for many days.

Then one day Elisha and a few other pancake hunters came back from the forest. The people who hired them were waiting anxiously for them, because their children wanted pancakes and they wanted them now! Elisha told the people, "Sorry, folks, no pancakes today. We looked all over the forest, and we didn't find a single nest. We saw no mother birds, we saw no eggs, and we are really tired, so that's the story." And that was the story the next day, too, and the next and the next.

Then one night God spoke to Elisha, waking him from a sound sleep. "You call yourself a pancake hunter?" God said. "Let me ask you something. Where do you think eggs come from?"

"From mother birds," Elisha answered in a soft, shaky voice, because when you are talking to God, if you can say anything, it usually comes out soft and shaky.

"And where do you think mother birds come from?" God asked Elisha.

"F-f-from eggs."

"*Bingo!*" said God. "And where do you think the eggs are going to come from to hatch into mother birds who will lay more eggs, if you take all the eggs and all the mother birds you can find? I have given you a good world with lots of food in it, but if you are going to act like pigs and eat it all up now, your children and your children's children will never have pancakes again! So be careful with all the animals and living things I have given you for food. If you eat them all today, you are going to go hungry tomorrow."

The very next morning, Elisha called all the pancake hunters together and told them, "New rules! From now on when we see a mother bird on a nest, we go back to the old way of scaring her away before we take the eggs. That way she can make new eggs, and we can have jobs, and the people can have pancakes, and God won't have to wake me up in the middle of a good night's sleep, telling me how I am a selfish pig and how we are eating all the food God gave us today and not leaving any for tomorrow." And all the pancake hunters agreed to the new rules—which were really the old rules that they had broken to make more money.

When Moses wrote down the laws in the law book, Elisha reminded Moses to write down the egg law: "If you see a bird's nest in a tree or on the ground and there are eggs or baby birds in the nest, and there is a mother bird sitting on the nest, do not take the mother bird and the eggs. You can take the eggs, but you can't take the eggs *and* the mother bird."

Elisha was happy, because after the egg law there were always enough eggs for pancakes; the mother birds were happy, because they always had more eggs than they could take care of; and God was happy, because in this little way some people had learned about taking care of living things today so that they would be alive tomorrow.

Then Elisha took a few friends, and they all went hunting for maple syrup.

—Deuteronomy 22:6

Ox Drool Bread

....

Moses was a very good man and a very smart man, but Moses had one big problem. For a long time in his life, Moses didn't listen to kids. He thought that kids had to grow up and become adults before they had anything important to say. Whenever a child had something to say, Moses would always interrupt the child, saying, "When you grow up, you will understand." Moses didn't even listen to his own son, Gershon, who was a very good and very smart kid, but that didn't matter to Moses. As far as Moses was concerned, children were supposed to be seen and not heard, and lots of times it was fine with Moses if they were not seen *or* heard.

Then one day Moses changed, and the reason was the ox drool bread. You see, all day, every day, people would come to Moses with problems, and he would have to decide what to do. One day a bunch of mothers came to Moses to complain. "Smell this bread!" they shouted as they shoved a piece of flat bread under Moses' nose.

Moses squinched up his nose and said, "Yuck! What's that smell?"

"That's the smell of ox drool, Mr. Moses!" one of the women explained. "Our bread has been coming out smelling like ox drool, and none of our kids will eat it. We hate it, too."

"How did the bread get this way?" Moses asked the women.

"Come with us to two-legged Fred, the flour-maker," one responded, "and you can see for yourself." So Moses and the women went to the place where two-legged Fred made flour out of wheat. People called the miller two-legged Fred because he had an ox who was also named Fred. To be able to tell them apart, they called Fred the ox four-legged Fred and they called Fred the human being two-legged Fred. One thing you learn as you grow up is that there are always a few really goofy people around.

Anyway, Moses and the women with the gripe about the ox drool bread saw four-legged Fred walking around and around in a circle on the rocks that crushed the hard outside of the wheat so that the soft inside could be ground up into flour. Everybody saw the problem right away. It was a hot day, and four-legged Fred was drooling huge globs of ox drool all over the wheat as he walked around the circle.

Moses screamed at two-legged Fred, "This is disgusting! Tie up the mouth of your stupid ox so he doesn't drool on the stupid wheat. I have big things to decide here, and I can't waste my time smelling ox drool bread!"

"I won't do it!" two-legged Fred said to Moses. "Four-legged Fred gets cool from his drool. The wind blows on the drool, and he gets cool because drying drool to Fred is like sweat for us. People sweat, oxen drool. That's the way it is! If I tie up his mouth, he will fall over dead from the heat, and I am not going to do it!"

Moses said, "Well, you better find some way to get the ox drool out of the bread, and you better find it soon!" Then Moses stomped off.

Gershon, Moses' son, had been tagging along behind his father. He pulled on Moses' pants and said in a little voice, "I have an idea, Daddy!"

Moses just brushed Gershon away and said, "Quiet, son, this is a big person's problem. You don't know anything about it."

Meanwhile, two-legged Fred was doing everything he could to solve the ox drool problem. The first thing he tried was an ox bib. But there was way too much drool for one bib.

Two-legged Fred's next idea was to hang a big umbrella under four-legged Fred's nose to catch the ox drool. This looked good until four-legged Fred shook himself. That's when the umbrella and a whole load of ox drool went flying all over the place.

Two-legged Fred tried all sorts of other ideas, but nothing worked. He tried fanning four-legged Fred to keep him cool, but he couldn't fan fast enough. He tried soaking four-legged Fred with buckets of water, but the water mixed with the ox drool and made things stink even worse.

By the end of the day, Moses came back to see how things were going, and he found two-legged Fred sitting on the crushing stones with his head in his hands, looking sad. "Sorry, Moses," he said. "I'm fresh out of ideas. I can't separate my ox from his drool. What can I do?"

Moses thought and then said, "I'm out of ideas, too. I'm good at figuring out how to get people out of Egypt, but I am not that good at figuring out how to get ox drool out of bread."

Then Gershon pulled on Moses' pants again and said in a louder voice, "Daddy, I have an idea!"

Moses pushed Gershon away and said, "Gershon, you are just a child and you don't understand." Gershon ran away, crying.

Moses left two-legged Fred, and on his way home saw his son sitting on a tree stump. Gershon was still crying. Moses went over to his son and asked him, "What's wrong, son?"

Gershon said through his tears, "A kid can have a good idea, too! God didn't give grown-ups all the brains, you know. Dad, you are such a dufus!"

Moses sat down next to Gershon and put his hand around his son and wiped away his tears. Moses was quiet for a while, and then he said to his son, "You're right. I'm sorry. Please tell me your idea. Please."

Gershon looked at his father and said, "Why don't you just grind the wheat at night?" Moses thought for a moment and let out a big laugh. He hugged Gershon, kissed him, and ran back to two-legged Fred. Moses called all the people together and said to them, "From now on we will grind the wheat at night! It's cooler at night, so four-legged Fred

won't drool as much as he does in the hot sun in the daytime. Two-legged Fred won't have to muzzle four-legged Fred, and we won't have to eat ox drool bread anymore."

Everyone cheered Moses, but he stopped the cheering and said, "You should all know that this great idea came from my son, Gershon. He was right. I have been a real dufus up to now. I thought children could not have good ideas, but I was wrong. From now on I am going to listen to what the children have to say. I won't always do what they say, but I promise to always listen."

Then all the kids cheered, and they went over to Gershon to pat him on the back and thank him. Two-legged Fred also thanked Gershon, and even four-legged Fred licked Gershon and smiled a kind of ox drool smile.

From that day on, the bread did not taste like ox drool, and everybody was happy. The next day Gershon and a whole group of children came to Moses with a new idea. Gershon said, "Daddy, we think that there should be chocolate served with every meal."

Moses laughed a happy laugh. He laughed, but he listened.

—Deuteronomy 25:4

God's
Mailbox

....

The best builder of anything in the Bible was a guy named Bezalel. Whenever something had to get built, the people in charge of building it *always* called on Bezalel to build it. Even God chose Bezalel to build all the important things God wanted built. Bezalel built a terrific seven-branched candlestick made of gold for the Temple in Jerusalem. Each one of the seven cups for the oil and the wick light looked like the flowers of an almond tree, and when the wicks were lit, they looked like little fireflies glowing inside seven golden flowers.

Bezalel's best work was the box to hold the Ten Commandments. The box was acacia wood covered in gold, and on top of the box were two golden angels whose big wings covered the whole thing. There were rings and poles on the side of the box to carry it around. The problem with the Ten Commandments box was that God told the people not to look at the box, because it was so special. A few people who did look at it had their faces melt off, and after that *nobody* wanted to look at the Ten Commandments box again. Bezalel was kind of sad about this, because the box was his best work, but he did understand that nobody wanted to get a face melt.

Because Bezalel was so good, the other artists and builders were jealous of him. Some would say behind his back, "Sure, Bezalel makes great things, but God gives him all the great designs. All Bezalel has to do is put them together."

Bezalel didn't care what people said. Bezalel was happy to give all the credit to God. "I am just God's hands," Bezalel would always say. But God was not happy that Bezalel was not getting enough credit for what he did, and so one day God did a very strange thing, even for God. God announced a contest. One day everybody saw pieces of paper floating down from the sky, and on each piece of paper there was this very strange announcement:

Build me a mailbox! Take a week to do it.

> Signed,
> God

Everybody was excited to build God a mailbox, and they scurried off to draw and hammer and nail and paint. All the big designers were working in secret, but even the children were building mailboxes for God. Everybody thought they had a chance to build the best mailbox for God, because God had not given out the design.

The next week came so fast that not everybody had finished their mailboxes by dawn, when the contest was to be decided. All the people who had finished their mailboxes had them covered up so that nobody else could see them, except for Dagliel, who was happy to show everybody his designs. One of Dagliel's mailboxes was a fish on a stick. This didn't work, because after one or two days, Dagliel's mailbox began to stink. Another design was a big blue mailbox with wings. This didn't work either, because Dagliel couldn't figure out how to move the wings.

When the contest really began, the first one to show his design for God's mailbox was Ziptor the grape grower. Ziptor's mailbox was a bunch of grape-colored balloons all tied with strings to a mailbox that had the name GOD painted on both sides. Hanging from the strings was also a card that read,

Dear God,
The prayers and letters in this mailbox have been lifted up to you

by Ziptor the grape grower. Any sunshine and good rain on our vineyards would be greatly appreciated!

Yours truly,
Ziptor

Ziptor was quite proud of his design and said, "My grape-balloon God mailbox will deliver prayers and packages to God faster than any other way. I am sure to win." Then Ziptor let go of the balloons, and they flew up into the sky. But birds pecked at the balloons and popped them, thinking that they were humongous grapes. Ziptor's mailbox crashed to the ground.

Then Baruch the sign painter uncovered his design for God's mailbox. It was a four-sided box with a red flag on top and huge signs painted on every side. One of the signs read, EAT ZIPTOR'S GRAPES AND GET A FREE BALLOON. Another sign said, COMING TO JERUSALEM FOR THE HOLIDAYS? WHY NOT STAY AT THE JERUSALEM GRAND HOTEL? WE PUT A CAMEL IN EVERY ROOM. Baruch explained that the signs were a new idea he had been working on, called advertising. He said, "I figure there will be lots of people coming to God's mailbox, and everybody will see the signs. I sold space on the mailbox for people who want to sell stuff to the folks bringing letters to God's mailbox." Nobody believed Baruch that folks would buy something just because they saw it on a pretty sign.

Then came Oholiab's turn. When he took the cover off the mailbox he had designed for God, people gasped. Some could not say a single word. Some just muttered, "Wow! Golly! Awesome!" Oholiab had built a golden tower. The tower had flags and bells and little carved animals and flowers decorating every part. The tower had small shelves and drawers and slots and clips for letters and packages, and the whole thing shimmered and tinkled in the wind like a great big chime. Nobody had ever seen anything more beautiful. Some people said, "It's more beautiful than the golden box Bezalel made to hold the Ten Commandments," but since none of them had ever looked at that box, it was hard to know

for sure. Everybody agreed that this was going to be the winner of God's mailbox contest for sure and that not even the great Bezalel could top the wonderful golden mailbox tower of Oholiab.

Then Bezalel removed the covering from his design. People started to laugh right away. Bezalel had made a pile of stones, just plain stones! He had not even cut them or carved them. He had just fitted them together to make a kind of a table of uncut stones. "Nice rocks!" someone called out to Bezalel. "Real nice rocks. You didn't even take the time to cut them so that they fit together right. What do you think you're doing? Where do you put the prayers and letters to God? Your mailbox is a joke!"

Bezalel waited for all the laughing to stop, and then he said in a quiet voice, "I made God's mailbox out of uncut stones for a whole bunch of reasons.

"I don't think God needs a mailbox that flies around in the air, so I made it out of things that are part of the earth. This way people will learn that God is not just high up in the sky but down here where we live.

"I did not make God's mailbox out of gold, because the only words that should be in a golden box are God's words to us, not our words to God. We already have a golden box for God's words, and that's enough.

"I did not make God's mailbox to be a place for selling things. God's mailbox is a place where we should remember to be happy with what we have, not a place where we should be tricked into wanting more.

"But most of all I decided to make God's mailbox out of uncut stones to teach people that what is true about stones is also true about people. Building with uncut stones is harder than building with stones you cut to fit, but it is better because you let each rock keep its own shape, and you don't cut off its edges just to make it fit. It's the same with people. It's harder and it takes more time to teach people how to work together than to just order them around and make them do things they do not understand. People who fit together to do a big job are even harder to find than stones that fit together to make a mailbox for God. But it's better to wait for the fit.

"These uncut stones remind us that the best things we build in this world are the things that leave everything whole. God gives each of us special edges and special gifts that are given to no other person in the whole wide world. Stones are different, too, until they are cut. But if we keep our edges and do the most with our gifts, then each and every one of us will be God's mailbox."

The people were quiet for a long time after Bezalel spoke. Some of them were crying and some of them were nodding and some just said, "Wow! Golly! Awesome!"

Then Oholiab said, "Bezalel, we were wrong about you. We thought you just had great hands. You also have a great heart. You can build stuff for us anytime."

Then the people put their letters and prayers on God's mailbox, and every letter and every prayer was answered.

—Deuteronomy 27:5–6

Epilogue

The Rainbow
People

....

Every day God saves the world because of one good person.

You see, every day as God looks at the mess we are making out of our world, God sees lots of reasons to make a new world with new people. God sees the world filled with hurting and stealing, with lying and cheating, with children starving and families sleeping in the street, with making war and making pollution, and with killing and more killing. Every day God sees lots of good reasons to make a new world with new people.

Now, of course, God did wipe out life on the world once already. In the time of Noah, God brought a great flood, but after the flood, God promised never to do it again. But God did not promise Noah that all life on earth would not be wiped out some *other* way. God did not promise Noah that a big fire or a big earthquake would not wipe out all life on earth. And God definitely did not promise Noah that a gigantic asteroid made of chocolate pudding would not crash into the earth and cover everything with chocolate pudding so thick that the world would just glop to an end. God promised Noah only that such a big flood would never come again. That's *all* God promised Noah.

Anyway, every day God sees the badness in the world and decides to destroy it, but then something happens. Every day, God sees some good person doing a good thing. Some days what God sees is a good person stopping a fight, or saving a child from a fire, or feeding a bunch of hungry folks, or building a house for a family with no money. Some days God sees a parent hugging a child or a child giving away some of his or her extra clothes to children with not a lot of clothes. When God sees any of these good people doing any of these or other good things, God thinks, It would not be fair to wipe out this goodness with all the badness. I am going to save the whole world today because of that person's good deed. That's how it goes every single day.

Now, there's just one catch: God has decided that a *different* good person has to save the world every day. One good person can save the world, but only for one day in his or her whole life, and that person never knows what day their good deed saved the world. It is not important that they know—it is only important that God knows. And God knows that *that* day, *that* person is the one who gave God *the* reason to let the world with all its badness live one more day, and to keep the gigantic chocolate pudding asteroid from glopping the earth. So that's the catch: *Each good person can save the world for only one day.*

Because the year has three hundred sixty-five days in it, the world needs three hundred sixty-five good-deed-doing people to save it every year. Because the deal with Noah was signed by God with a rainbow, the good people who save the world are called by God the rainbow people.

After Noah, there were thousands and thousands of rainbow people whose good deeds saved the world. Right after the flood, Noah's family were the rainbow people who saved the world for a while, mostly by helping animals who were stuck in the mud and by helping each other find food in the drying-out earth. Later on, their children and their children's children's children became rainbow people, and they spread all over the world, so that, in time, there were rainbow people doing good deeds in every country. And in every religion and in every color of skin and in both sexes and in every kind of person who could ever be, there were enough rainbow people to save the world by a single good deed every day.

Moses was a rainbow person. He saved the world on the day when he was tending the sheep of his father-in-law, Jethro, and one of the sheep ran away from the flock. Moses started to follow the sheep who

was running away when the other shepherds said, "Let that one go, Moses. Catching her will be hard, and the rest of the flock needs you. She isn't worth the trouble. She is wolf food now. Let her go."

But Moses did not listen to the other shepherds. He went after that runaway sheep and brought her back to her mother. God was watching Moses that day and said, "Because Moses cared enough about one single sheep, I know Moses will care about *all* my people. I will make Moses the one who will take my people out of slavery in Egypt, and because of his good deed in getting that sheep, I will save the whole world today."

Jesus was a rainbow person. One day Jesus went over to a woman nobody would talk to. She had done some bad things but was sorry for them. He became her friend, and because people loved Jesus, they forgave that woman and were nice to her again. On that day, God saved the world because of Jesus.

The Buddha was a rainbow person. One day the Buddha gave everything he owned to poor people, becoming a poor person himself, to help all people learn that it is not what you have but what you are that counts. The day the Buddha gave up all his stuff, God saved the world because of the Buddha.

Muhammad was a rainbow person. One day Muhammad was asked what the most important teaching of God was, and he took that person to feed a hungry person right then and right there, and on that day when Muhammad fed the hungry person, God saved the world because of Muhammad.

Moses, Jesus, the Buddha, and Muhammad were all very famous rainbow people. Whole new religions came from their teachings and from their good deeds, but remember God's rainbow rule: *Each good person can save the world for only one day.* This means that in all the days and all the years the world has been alive, there has been one rainbow person, each and every day, whose good deed has saved the world. Some of them were famous—like Moses, Jesus, the Buddha, and Muhammad— and some were just ordinary good people doing ordinary good deeds, but for God none of these people and none of their deeds are ordinary. They are the ones who keep the world alive.

And here is the big news: *Each of you could be a rainbow person, too!* God needs a new rainbow person and a new good deed every day to keep the world alive. So the next time you can stop a fight, or feed a hungry person, or save an animal, or hug a person who has no friends, or kiss your parents, or share your toys, or give away a blanket or a coat in the wintertime to somebody who is out there freezing in the cold, or try to stop the killing in a faraway place where you don't even know anybody, or pick up a beer can by the road and bring it to a recycling center, or sing Happy Birthday to somebody who hasn't heard it for lots of years, or call your mother for no reason at all except to say that you love her and cannot ever thank her enough for raising you up to be a good person, or keep somebody from giving up hope that tomorrow will be a better day—whenever you do any of these things, or more, then, just *maybe*, you might be the rainbow person whose good deed saved the world that day from the humongous chocolate pudding asteroid just waiting to glop the earth on the day there are no rainbow people left.

So never give up, never lose hope, and never forget:

Every day God saves the world because of one good person, and today that good person could be you!

—*Genesis 6:9*